Roberte Ce Soir

and

The Revocation
of the
Edict of Nantes

PIERRE KLOSSOWSKI

Translated by
Austryn Wainhouse

Marion Boyars
New York · London

Republished paperback in 1989 by Marion Boyars Publishers
24 Lacy Road, London SW15 1NL
26 East 33rd Street, New York, NY 10016

Originally published by Les Editions de Miniut, France as
Roberte Ce Soir and *La Révocation de l'Edit de Nantes* in 1953 and 1959

British Library Cataloguing in Publication Data
Klossowski, Pierre
  Roberte ce soir; and, The revocation
  of the Edict of Nantes
  I. Title II. Klossowski, Pierre.
  Revocation of the Edict of Nantes
  III. La revocation de L'Edit de Nantes.

  843'.914 [F]

Library of Congress Cataloging-in-Publication Data

Klossowski, Pierre.
  [Roberte ce soir. English]
  Roberte ce soir: and, The revocation of the edict of Nantes/
  Pierre Klossowski; translated by Austryn Wainhouse.
    p. cm.
  Translation of: Roberte ce soir, and La Révocation de l'édit de
Nantes.
    1. Klossowski, Pierre–Translations, English. 2. Erotic stories, French–Translations into English. 3. Erotic stories, English–Translations from French. I. Klossowski, Pierre. Révocation de l'edit de Nantes. English. 1988. II. Title. III. Title: Roberte ce soir. IV. Title: Revocation of the edict of Nantes.
PQ2621.L6A27 1988
843' .912–dc19   88–16692

ISBN 0–7145–2739–4

Printed and bound in Great Britain by
Biddles Ltd, Guildford and King's Lynn

Roberte Ce Soir

. . . cujus abditis adhuc
vitiis congruebat.

—Tacitus

My Uncle Octave, the eminent professor of scholastics at the University of Y***, suffered from his conjugal happiness as though from an illness, firm in the belief he would be cured of it once he had made it contagious. My Aunt Roberte's beauty was of that sober sort which so often conceals pronounced tendencies to frivolity: discovering them, you feel wronged and regret not having proceeded somewhat more purposefully. Strangely enough, my uncle considered himself the foremost victim of this equivocal situation; my aunt realized it, and had become that much more rigid in her hostile attitude toward all his ideas. And the more she entrenched herself in this attitude, the more enigmatic my uncle judged her to be; searching a way out of his perplexity he had hit upon nothing better than to introduce into their way of life a rule of hospitality which our traditions condemn as shameful. My aunt passed for an "emancipated" woman, but here again my uncle was wrong; she of course could not do otherwise than disapprove of my uncle's innovation; but, and this is equally certain, she had been more than once obliged to fall in with the established custom. This, today, is how I account for the atmosphere in the house where I spent such a trying adolescence. My aunt treated me like a brother, and the professor had turned me into his favorite disciple; I served as a pretext for the practice of that hospitality which was practiced at my aunt's expense.

I was thirteen when my relatives adopted me. My uncle thought it necessary I be given a tutor, and I had a series of three, all chosen from among his and my aunt's acquaintances. They used to have a good many visitors at their summer home. This or that guest would suddenly be declared responsible for my education; a few months later, sometimes a few weeks later, he would disappear.

It is true enough that Aunt Roberte had aroused a storm of emotions in me. But my uncle, having correctly guessed what the matter was, took perfidious advantage of it in order to contemplate his own perversity at work in me. As with most boys at that age, my passion strove along thoroughly platonic lines. My uncle managed to transform it into a perfect nest of vipers, I don't know how else to describe the awful tangle of carnal and spiritual desires which the mental torture he inflicted upon me shortly had seething inside my breast. But that part of the story seems to me of only limited interest; on the other hand, since the professor's behavior demonstrates into what kind of pitfall language can lure even the most lucid intelligence, I have thought it worthwhile to note certain of his digressions and to reproduce them in the context of this extraordinary experience of my student years.

DIFFICULTIES

When my Uncle Octave took my Aunt Roberte in his arms, one must not suppose that in taking her he was alone. An invited guest would enter while Roberte, entirely given over to my uncle's presence, was not expecting him, and while she was in fear lest the guest arrive—for with irresistible resolution Roberte awaited the arrival of some guest —the guest would already be looming up behind her as my uncle made his entry just in time to surprise my aunt's satisfied fright at being surprised by the guest. But in my uncle's mind it was all over and done with in the twinkling of an eye, and once again my uncle would be on the point of taking my aunt in his arms. It would be over in the twinkling of an eye . . . for, after all, one cannot at the same time take and not take, be there and not be there, enter a room when one is already in it. My Uncle Octave would have been asking too much had he wished to prolong the instant of the opened door, he was already doing exceedingly well in getting the guest to appear in the doorway at the precise moment he did, getting the guest to loom up behind Roberte so that he, Octave, might be able to sense that he himself was the guest as, borrowing from the guest his door-opening gesture, he could behold them from the threshold and have the impression it was he, Octave, who was taking my aunt by surprise.

Nothing could give a better idea of my uncle's mentality

than these hand-written pages he had framed under glass and then hung on the wall of the guest room, just above the bed, a spray of fading wildflowers drooping over the old-fashioned frame.

THE RULE OF HOSPITALITY

The master of this house, having no greater nor more pressing concern than to shed the warmth of his joy at evening upon whomever comes to dine at his table and to rest under his roof from a day's wearying travel, waits anxiously at the gate for the stranger he will see appear like a liberator upon the horizon. And catching a first glimpse of him in the distance, though he be still far off, the master will call out to him, "Come in quickly, my happiness is at stake." This is why the master will be grateful in advance to anybody who, rather than considering hospitality as an accident in the souls of him and of her who offer it, shall take it as the very essence of the host and hostess, the stranger in his guest's capacity partaking of this essence. For with the stranger he welcomes, the master of the house seeks a no longer accidental, but an essential relationship. At the start the two are but isolated substances, between them there is none but accidental communication: you who believe yourself far from home in the home of someone you believe to be at home, you bring merely the accidents of your substance, such accidents as conspire to make a stranger of you, to him who bids you avail yourself of all that makes a merely accidental host of him. But because the master of this house herewith invites the stranger to penetrate to the source of all substances beyond the realm of all accident, this is how he inaugurates a substantial relationship between himself and the stranger, which will be not a relative relationship but an absolute one, as though, the master becoming one with the stranger, his relationship with you who have just set foot here were now but a relationship of one with oneself.

To this end the host translates himself into the actual guest. Or, if you prefer, he actualizes a possibility of the guest quite as you, the guest, actualize a possibility of the host. The host's most eminent gratification has for its object the actualization in the mistress of the house of the inactual essence of the hostess. Now upon whom is this duty incumbent if not upon the guest? Does this mean that the master of the house might expect betrayal at the hands of the mistress of the house? Now it seems that the essence of the hostess, such as the host visualizes it, would in this sense be undetermined and contradictory. For either the essence of the hostess is constituted by her fidelity to the host, and in this case she eludes him the more he wishes to know her in the opposite state of betrayal, for she would be unable to betray him in order to be faithful to him; or else the essence of the hostess is really constituted by infidelity and then the host would cease to have any part in the essence of the hostess who would be susceptible of belonging, accidentally, as mistress of the house, to some one or other of the guests. The notion of mistress of the house reposes upon an existential basis; she is a hostess only upon an essential basis: this essence is therefore subjected to restraint by her actual existence as mistress of the house. And here the sole function of betrayal, we see, is to lift this restraint. If the essence of the hostess lies in fidelity to the host, this authorizes the host to cause the hostess, essential in the existent mistress of the house, to manifest herself before the eyes of the guest; for the host in playing host must accept the risks of the game, and these include the consequences of his wife's strict application of the rules of hospitality and of the fact that she dare not be unmindful of her essence, composed of fidelity to the host, for fear that in the arms of the inactual guest come here to actualize her *qua* hostess, the mistress of the household exist only traitorously.

If the essence of the hostess lay in infidelity, the outcome of the game would be a foregone conclusion and the host the loser before it starts. But the host wishes to experience the risk of losing and feels that losing rather than winning in advance, he will, at whatever the cost, grasp the essence of the hostess in the infidelity of the mistress of the house. For to possess the faithless one *qua* hostess faithfully fulfilling her duties, that is what he is after. Hence by means of the guest he wishes to actualize something potential in the mistress of the house: an actual hostess in relation to this guest, an inactual mistress of the house in relation to the host.

If the hostess' essence remains thus indeterminate, because to the host it seems that something of the hostess might escape him in the event this essence were nothing but pure fidelity on the part of the mistress of the house, the essence of the host is proposed as a homage of the host's curiosity to the essence of the hostess. Now this curiosity, as a potentiality of the hospitable soul, can have no proper existence except in that which would look to the hostess, were she naive, like suspicion or jealousy. The host however is neither suspicious nor jealous, because he is essentially curious about that very thing which, in everyday life, would make a master of the house suspicious, jealous, unbearable.

Let the guest not be the least bit uneasy; above all let him not suppose he could ever constitute the cause for any jealousy or suspicion when there is not even anyone to feel these sentiments. In reality the guest is anything but that; for it is owing to the absence of cause for jealousy and suspicion, which are not otherwise determined than by this absence, that the guest is going to emerge from his stranger's accidental relationship to enjoy an essential relationship with the hostess whose essence he shares with the host. The host's essence—hospitality—rather than being confined to impulses of jealousy or suspicion, aspires to convert into a presence the absence of cause of these impulses, and to actualize itself in that cause. Let the guest understand his role well: let him then fearlessly excite the host's curiosity by that jealousy and that suspicion, worthy in the master of the house but unworthy of a host; the latter enjoins the guest loyally to do his utmost; in this competition let them surpass each other in subtlety: let the host put the guest's discretion to the test, the guest make proof of the host's curiosity: the term generosity has no place here, it is without meaning in the discussion, since everything is generosity, and everything is also greed; but let the guest take all due care lest this jealousy or this suspicion grow to such proportions in the host that no room is left for his curiosity; for it is upon this curiosity the guest will depend in order to display his abilities.* If the host's curiosity aspires to actualize itself in the absent cause, how does he hope to convert this absence into presence unless it be that he awaits the visitation of an angel? Solicited by the host's piety, the angel is capable of concealing himself in the guise of a guest—is it you?—whom the host believes fortuitous. To what extent will the angel actualize in the

---

* But here a new element enters into the picture, here opens a new phase: realizing that to attain his ends he needs means which concrete life does not afford, Uncle Octave goes off to hunt for them in the obscurest mysticism. (*Antoine's note.*)

mistress of the house the essence of the hostess such as the host is prone to visualize it, when this essence is known to none but him who beyond all being knows? By inclining the host farther and farther, for the guest, be he angel or no, is only inclination in the host: learn, dear guest, that neither the host, nor yourself, nor again the hostess herself yet knows the essence of the hostess; surprised by you she will attempt to find herself in the host who then will no longer hold her back: but who, knowing her in your arms, will hold himself richer in his treasure than ever.

In order that the host's curiosity not degenerate into jealousy or suspicion, it is for you, the guest, to discern the hostess' essence in the mistress of the house, for you to cast her forth from potentiality into existence: either the hostess remains sheer phantasm and you a stranger in this house if you leave to the host the inactualized essence of the hostess; or else you are indeed that angel, and by your presence you give an actuality to the hostess: you shall have full power over her as well as over the host. And so, cherished guest, you cannot help but see that it is in your best interest to fan the host's curiosity to the point where the mistress of the house, driven out of herself, will be completely actualized in an existence which shall be determined by you alone, by you, the guest, and not by the host's curiosity. Whereupon the host shall be master in his house no more: he shall have carried out his mission. In his turn he shall have become the guest.

I
THE DENUNCIATION

Allez, allez, Madame,
Etaler vos appas et vanter vos mépris
A l'infâme sorcier qui charme vos esprit.

—Corneille, *Médée*, II

In Octave's study. Evening.
Octave and Antoine, his nephew.

ANTOINE
Have you developed more pictures of your stay at Ascona, Uncle Octave?

OCTAVE
Look at this one. Quite a success, wouldn't you say?

ANTOINE
Where on earth did you take it?

OCTAVE
In Madame de Watteville's villa where the debates were held.

ANTOINE
What an extraordinary scene . . . this young lady . . .

OCTAVE
. . . whose skirt is starting to burn and who leaps away from the fireplace and into the arms of this gentleman who has rushed up to her rescue and is snatching off her burning clothes.

ANTOINE

But it's Aunt Roberte! . . . Come now, uncle, you've faked it somehow, haven't you? You don't mean to say this is a picture of something that actually happened?

OCTAVE

I snapped it while your aunt was in the midst of delivering her lecture in the living room of the villa. While speaking she carelessly leaned her elbow on the mantelpiece, and the next moment her skirt caught fire.

ANTOINE

And all you could think of was to take a picture of her at a time like that?

OCTAVE

I tell you I had my camera out to photograph her giving her speech, and just as I was ready to click the shutter the incident occurred. . . .

ANTOINE

The accident, Uncle Octave.

OCTAVE

The incident, I tell you.

ANTOINE

Will you give me a copy of this photo, Uncle Octave?

OCTAVE

Quite out of the question. It's vital to an operation I might however be prepared to let you in on if you're sure you can hold your tongue.

ANTOINE

Word of honor.

OCTAVE

But before anything else I should have to ask you some rather pointed questions.

ANTOINE

Uncle Octave, I should be only too happy—

OCTAVE

You must realize from the start that once they are asked you are going to be less free, even if you refuse to answer.

ANTOINE

What good is my freedom? I don't know what to use it for. Hearing you say what I don't dare admit to myself will be a relief for me. Your words will give me a clearer image of myself.

OCTAVE

At this very moment someone is standing between you, my nephew, and me, your uncle.

ANTOINE

Someone standing between us? Good lord, have things gone that far already?

OCTAVE

It is not your Aunt Roberte I have in mind . . . nor am I thinking of our disputes revolving around the problem of your education.

ANTOINE

Oh! . . . Why then . . .

OCTAVE
(*as though waiving an objection*)
But someone is there all the same. Someone who may none the less have a hand to play in your schooling.

ANTOINE

But between you and me? Who else is there, Uncle Octave?

OCTAVE

He who even now is preventing us from understanding each other.

ANTOINE

What do you mean?

OCTAVE

And yet without him we'd not be able to bring this off.

ANTOINE

Some fourth person is involved?

OCTAVE

No, a third, he who intrudes between you and me, between me and Aunt Roberte, between your aunt and yourself.

ANTOINE

This is very disturbing. . . .

OCTAVE

And this third person is a pure spirit.

ANTOINE

You're joking!

OCTAVE

I have never been more serious. I have *named Roberte* to him.

ANTOINE
(*puzzled*)

Whatever are you aiming at?

OCTAVE

Simply at fulfilling your desires.

ANTOINE
(*startled*)

You . . . my . . . with my aunt?

OCTAVE
(*reassuring him*)

Don't rush to any conclusions. Nothing is more . . . impalpable in spite of appearances. . . . Everything depends on the spirit.

ANTOINE

Uncle Octave, is there something wrong?

OCTAVE

It's as I feared, you are still lacking in discernment.

ANTOINE

Then help me acquire it.

OCTAVE

Then listen carefully to me. I named Roberte to the pure spirit.

ANTOINE

You have already said so, and it's just that I can't figure out. How could you name her to a pure spirit?

OCTAVE

Don't bother yourself with doubts of the possibility of doing something that has been done. And there is no undoing it now. You have got to accept things as they are, Antoine, otherwise it will be useless for us to continue.

ANTOINE

All right, let's say I accept it. But do please explain this to me.

OCTAVE

Along with being obtuse you are in a dreadful hurry to find out the consequences of something of which you so far haven't the faintest notion. The mere fact I made a denunciation to the pure spirit isn't what should have struck you; but—and this is serious, no less serious than the talk we are having now—that instead of naming the spirit to Roberte, as my relations with her would ordinarily have led us to expect, the reverse took place. Unbeknown to your Aunt Roberte, I, your Uncle Octave, denounce my wife to a pure spirit. Whereupon Roberte is made the *object* of a pure spirit, the latter thereupon becoming my accomplice.

ANTOINE

I understand that as we are talking here my aunt is the object of our conversation, of our thoughts, as would be anybody or anything else we happened to be discussing, including this pure spirit. But how can my aunt become the object of that spirit's preoccupations?

OCTAVE

Don't say "my aunt." Say "Roberte" and you will see it at once. For when you think of your aunt, in the way you think of her and I know in what way you think of her, as do I, you think simply of Roberte.

ANTOINE

Yes. There's no keeping anything from you.

OCTAVE

So repeat what I just said to you.

ANTOINE

My Uncle Octave named my Aunt Roberte to the pure spirit.

OCTAVE

But not at all! That isn't what I said. Once again: I have named Roberte to the pure spirit. Repeat it exactly.

ANTOINE

I have named Roberte to the pure spirit.

OCTAVE

Right you are, and you did so the moment you began to think of her, although with one difference, to wit that, no

more than does your aunt, you haven't the precise notion of
the pure spirit which would enable you to invoke him. But
as regards Roberte you believe you have a very clear image.

ANTOINE

Mine's surely not as well defined as yours, Uncle Octave.

OCTAVE

You are mistaken there. For the fact is Roberte eludes me
to the point where I am obliged to invoke the pure spirit.
Bringing her to his attention, she becomes the object of his
attention, in his attention to her there is revealed to me what
she hides from me—and which she may perhaps not hide
from you. Well?

ANTOINE

For me Aunt Roberte is a kind of elder sister, attentive and
severe at the same time.

OCTAVE
(*a hint of worry in his manner*)
And nothing else?

ANTOINE

Condescending if not contemptuous when it comes to the
theology lessons you give me.

OCTAVE

Yes, yes, the picture holds together.

ANTOINE

Unbelieving and austere, I might add.

OCTAVE

Unbelief for me, austerity for you. And is that the whole of Roberte? Is this she who can become the object of the pure spirit? Form and content, actual and inactual? Tell me, my boy, which shall we designate to the pure spirit, her unbelief or her austerity?

ANTOINE

"We designate"? Aren't you the one who is doing it in naming her to the pure spirit?

OCTAVE

Which would you designate, Antoine, if you were in my place?

ANTOINE

Her unbelief.

OCTAVE

Rubbish!

ANTOINE

You ask me: in your place . . .

OCTAVE

You yourself would therefore denounce her austerity.

ANTOINE
(*dodging the issue*)

Once you name her to the pure spirit, aren't you denouncing the whole of Roberte to him?

OCTAVE

Between naming and denouncing there is a notable difference. In Roberte it is not the dutiful helpmate I would denounce, it's that in her which, lurking behind all the little helpfulnesses performed and duties fulfilled, perpetrates great wrongs, steals in the act of giving and can't be found out because the helpmate activities cover up the evidence. (*Octave forgets he is speaking to his nephew; the latter begins to shuffle his feet uncomfortably; Octave catches himself, then resumes.*) What I denounced to the pure spirit is not the everyday actuality of our conjugal life but that very inactuality the pure spirit shares with Roberte.

ANTOINE

Then if Roberte's inactuality is already shared by the pure spirit, you merely designate to him something about her that he already knows?

OCTAVE

By way of answering your question I might ask you this one: didn't you say that for you your aunt is like an elder sister, attentive and severe at the same time?

ANTOINE

I did.

OCTAVE

Attentiveness and severity are things you grasp in her whereas I do not; they are inactual for me, actual for you.

ANTOINE

Granted.

OCTAVE

And didn't you go on to say that she is somewhat contemptuous of my most serious studies?

ANTOINE

I said that too.

OCTAVE

And just a moment ago didn't you sum up your impressions in calling her unbelieving and austere?

ANTOINE

I did indeed.

OCTAVE

All this—tell me, is it actual for me or for you?

ANTOINE

It's exactly how my aunt appears in my mind.

OCTAVE

In your mind. So here is a part of my wife's inactuality revealed to me: the "attentive and severe elder sister" posture she adopts as regards my nephew. Tell me now, what lies behind these figures of speech? Is this the impression an aunt customarily gives to her nephew?

ANTOINE

No, I don't suppose so.

OCTAVE

As for her unbelief, I know all about that. But what am I to make of this austerity you ascribe to her?

ANTOINE

That's an unfortunate term.

OCTAVE

Could it be your way of indirectly referring to your pique?

(*Antoine is silent*)

She looks austere to you because her unbelief does not lead her to loose behavior?

ANTOINE

Maybe.

OCTAVE

But you none the less hold out hope of some loose behavior from her?

(*Antoine is silent again*)

Still, everything about her encourages you to anticipate such misbehavior?

ANTOINE

It's simply a mental picture I have of her.

OCTAVE

And now I can reply to the question you asked a little while ago: if this austerity is something you mentally picture, as this unbelief is something pictured in my own mind, these minds of ours are never sufficiently detached from our contingencies to enable us to judge and discover the underlying Roberte we seek: we designate this austerity to the pure spirit, it is foreign to him, certainly just as foreign as Roberte's inactuality. For the only inactuality that is familiar to you is that she is unbelieving and that your desires cannot exploit this quality as you would like. From this you conclude she is austere—and I, that she is faithful. Hence how could we help but designate to the pure spirit what lies behind her unbelief, the unbelief evident to our minds?

ANTOINE
(all of a sudden derisive, and authoritatively)
What else would you have there behind her unbelief if not the impossibility of the least relation ever being established between Roberte and the pure spirit?

OCTAVE
That argument looks sound to you; you fail to notice that instead of getting back of her unbelief you stop short of it. Were it Roberte's unbelief that creates the impossibility of establishing a relation between Roberte and the pure spirit, it would be futile to invoke the latter with a view to having him reveal the inactuality of Roberte which escapes us and which is nothing other than her essence. But if we are to hope to grasp her essence in this revelation of the pure spirit, we are obliged to suppose that, far from being at its origin, the unbelief merely follows from the impossibility founding it. That is why Roberte's austerity seems impossible to you. But in order to bring its falsity to light and to gain the upper hand over the impossible, one must first affirm that the impossibility *is,* which enables austere unbelief to exist.

ANTOINE
This is rather a shock: impossibility would be Roberte's inactuality. How could the pure spirit make it his object,

Uncle Octave, even if you do designate it to him? Where do we get from saying that impossibility *is?* Truly, I see no communication possible between Roberte and the spirit.

OCTAVE

The less you see, dear boy, the nearer you approach the truth: you see no possible communication of her nature for the reason that you fancy Roberte is always Roberte. Do you remember, when we were studying the mystery of hypostatic union, the basic principle which makes a person out of a reasoning substance? Think back for a moment upon all those subtleties of the Doctors we passed in review to explain this union of human nature and divine nature. Leaving aside their various interpretations, what was the one condition upon which they all agreed in regarding as fundamental to a conception of this union?

ANTOINE

The loss of the incommunicability proper to human nature.

OCTAVE

And, to begin with, what is incommunicability?

ANTOINE

The principle according to which the being of an individual cannot be attributed to several individuals, and which properly constitutes the person identical unto himself.

OCTAVE

What now is the privative function of the person?

ANTOINE

That of rendering our substance incapable of being assumed by a nature either lower or higher than ours.

OCTAVE

Is there a situation in which the reasoning substance loses personal incommunicability?

ANTOINE

To be sure, when our substance, composed of a body and a soul, is dissociated by death.

OCTAVE

And what then happens to the soul?

ANTOINE

It once again becomes capable of associating with a body.

OCTAVE

As a consequence, the separated but subsisting soul loses personal incommunicability, as shown by the fact it recovers its capacity to unite itself to a body. Now, may we imagine an operation occurring in the actual person whereby, dissociating the soul from the body and the spirit from the soul, the actual person is placed in suspense?

ANTOINE

In certain extreme cases, such as possession or ecstasy.

OCTAVE

And what must we conclude from this?

ANTOINE

That while our person renders us incapable of being associated to a nature either inferior or superior to our own, this same suspension of the person may however occur if God permits it to be so.

OCTAVE

Quite. Thus it stands established that before becoming incapable of whatever assumption by the personal actuality, every created substance and in particular every reasoning substance, considered as human nature, remains susceptible of one such assumption by another nature. And so it is that hypostatic union, which, as a mystery, cannot of course serve us as an example, has none the less furnished us, inadvertently as it were, the argument of personal incommunicability as well as the loss of the same. A reasoning substance considered as individuality could very well not be actual in itself. A human nature could once be assumed by a divine person. This human nature was none the less an individuality. Hence this individuality had no personal actuality in itself. Why?

ANTOINE

Uncle Octave, I'm afraid I don't know.

OCTAVE

Because an individuality, whether of human substance or spiritual, has no existence from the mere fact of being an essence, and this human nature consequently had no actuality other than that of a divine person. Now, what would happen to a human nature in whom a contrary impulse such as unbelief has suspended the incommunicable character? Must it not fall back into a state of essence without existence, as some have it, or, as others have it, into existence without essence, and in either case into this dependence which renders it assumable by another nature superior to its own? We would here appear to be faced by a dreadful hypostatic union. Roberte would be unbelieving only to the extent she repudiated her actuality in our midst and would be austere only to the extent her body permitted her to dissimulate the loss of her incommunicable character, susceptible as she would henceforth be to unite with whatever nature eager to actualize itself in her and hence to actualize her for herself.

ANTOINE
This nature eager to actualize itself in Roberte would then be no other than the pure spirit?

OCTAVE
The pure spirit is inactual in relation to me just as in relation to Roberte: inactual in relation to himself, so he remains up until the instant I invoke him for the purpose of designating the inactual Roberte to him, then and only then does he become actual. Previous to this the inactual Roberte could not be known to the pure spirit: but while we continue in ignorance of Roberte, once she is designated to him not only does he know what escapes me but he will himself be the actualization of inactual Roberte.

ANTOINE
What difference is there between us and the pure spirit as regards this inactuality of Roberte's? Why not simply say that we ourselves actualize in our relations with her that which is inactual in Roberte?

OCTAVE

Because we never do it without her knowledge! Whereas in designating her to the pure spirit who merges with her inactuality, it is without her being aware of it we enter into relation with the inactual Roberte. To date, you have known the inactual Roberte only in her "attentive and severe sister, unbelieving and austere" guise, and I in her guise of the dutiful wife. It's none other than the former I have denounced to the pure spirit, it is unbeknown to the latter the pure spirit is going to actualize what Roberte is alone in knowing with him. In fact, Roberte does not at all know in relation to me or in relation to you what she very well knows in relation to the pure spirit. So long as the pure spirit did not know her she did not know what she knows with him, just as he did not know what at present he knows with her.

ANTOINE

But in what way would this photograph be vital to such an operation?

OCTAVE

Hand it back to me and we shall project it on that screen which you may unroll. We place our projector here. Now, Antoine, kindly turn off the ceiling lights and pay attention. (*The scene in the de Watteville villa living room flashes upon the screen.*)

ANTOINE

It's wonderful. . . .

OCTAVE

Never mind telling me it's wonderful. Just describe what you see. Calmly.

ANTOINE

That magnificent mirror over the mantelpiece reflecting
the light from crystal chandeliers, all these people . . . in
the foreground, Aunt Roberte, panic-stricken . . .

OCTAVE

(*switching off the projector lamp*)

Aunt Roberte? Snap out of it, young man. Once again.
(*The image reappears upon the screen.*) What do you see?

ANTOINE

Roberte's panic-stricken face—although she is lifting her
head, her gaze still lingers on the hem of her skirt, which is
on fire, as is shown by that glaring patch of light . . . her
upraised right hand, its fingers widespread, indicates her
terror as her wrist is seized by that young gentleman she is
hugging to her bosom while he, as though brandishing a
torch, is tearing away the blazing part of the skirt, unveiling
the whole length of the leg she has bent at the knee, bent so
sharply the calf is touching her thigh—and that thigh is
amply in sight, for, my stars, there in her panties is the
outline of her bottom; the movement of this line traced
through the bent waist and continued through the bent knee
to the tip of her toes contrasts with the stiffness of the other
leg, braced hard, and eloquently expresses her fear of being
touched by the flames, while in the sidelong glance she is
about to throw upon her rescuer's powerful arm one seems to
detect a hint of amazement at the resolution of this gesture
which is thus baring her person, as is confirmed by the effort
she seems to be making, with her left hand, to check his
zeal. Very strange, this face divided between expressions of
alarm and surprise, these motions frozen in mid-flight, this

scrambling haste in suspense, this fluttering hand and the sinuous forms of the legs brought to a sudden halt—while as for him, all you see is his back. . . .

OCTAVE
(ruminating, while his nephew remains rapt in his contemplation of the scene)

Troubling case. . . . Here we are dealing not with a divine mystery but a counter-mystery or, if you like, a mystification; not that it is a question of illusion: mystification counterfeits mystery and presupposes it; its consequences, however, are no less grave for those it involves; as grave for Roberte as for us. To be sure, I could give other interpretations and work forward from another point of departure; divine essence expresses itself in three persons who are not three essences but a single essence, since there is only one divine essence. And each of them is at all times that essence in which each person is established as an essential relationship. With created beings, on the other hand, this relationship is merely accidental, and from one created nature to another, from one person to the next, there is no communication of essence like the intercommunication of the three persons within divine nature. To what extent would the human soul's essence, withdrawing from personal existence, recover the power to multiply itself in several persons or to express itself in as many persons as there were various subjects to perceive it *qua* object of participation? Would not this essence then have to be able to maintain itself, or be able to be maintained, as form? In relation to itself, this essence, actualized with each of its successive acts of consciousness by each external perception it were the object of, would see an internal relationship established inside itself. Suppose that

between you, me, and a third person, Roberte reproduces
within herself her relationship to all three of us; these inwardly reproduced relationships reflect not our own images
of her but, instead, the three different images of her we each
respectively form of her; a triple relationship to Roberte is
constituted in her own spirit: and now she is in three persons.
But in the three realizations that produce these three persons,
is the share of consciousness such as to warrant the assertion
that these three Robertes are also of a single essence? No, for
this trinity is wholly exterior to her, it comes to her only from
our outside presence. This triple representation of herself to
herself is hence not essential; the three Robertes are only
accidental in their relationship to Roberte, because this triple
representation of herself originates with us, and because it is
we alone who modify it; that these three Robertes be of a
single substance the minimum requirement would be that
the absolute Roberte know a Roberte-to-Roberte relationship
based upon her essence, that the three Robertes consummate
a single secret. If the conscious realization of Roberte by
Roberte—Roberte apprehending herself as particularized by
the judgment of others (which incites her to set her skirt
ablaze in order that someone expose her under the pretense
of saving her from the fire)—if one such act of consciousness is an act of her intelligence leaving room for other judg-
ments or other intentions whereof she would be that many
times the object, this act none the less remains an event whose
intimate connections are not with created being but with the
intellect prior to any creation—provided, that is, we adopt
Hochheim's thesis, according to which intelligence is of itself
something increate. Following this tack, we at once find
Roberte disposed to yield us her secret. If Roberte—insofar
as this name designates only a relationship to us, as it does

to what lies hidden behind that name—ceases indeed to be *that* Roberte to become momentarily *this* Roberte, the object of the judgment, of the intention, of the desire of others; if she ceases to be, I say, not without presupposing the Roberte-in-relationship-to-us—since she could not otherwise discern another Roberte in herself, the object of foreign designs—and were as a consequence to begin to lose her incommunicable character and take on the capacity to enter into composition with another nature, reverting into the state of uninformed substance or the state of nonactualized but simply actualizable form—; she would still come into conflict with her own body as with the equivocal witness of her presence among us, of her identity about to become false; she will only the more surely surrender her body to the condition of the actualizable. Well, all these facts are so many operations of intellection over which her fully conscious mind presides. Directly the intelligence involved were increate, it would here concern a created subject; but this subject, Roberte by name, would be in the service of the increate intelligence present in the operation. What then is happening here, if not that, in disactualizing herself as Roberte, whose skirt is accidentally on fire, Roberte's spirit is actualizing itself in as much as it provokes the gesture of another, who unveils her, by means of this disactualization! Into creatable existence the increate intelligence rejects the subject in whom this same action is taking place, and from this negation of a subject by its own consciousness there results a subjectless consciousness; but the term "consciousness" is ill applied to the absence of a subject; who then is here *cum scientia*? That something increate which intellect is. Now, as it is no less increate in a created suppositum, it begins, in this subject, by posing itself as an object because recreatable in its increate self. In this act

Roberte performs, increate intellect appears to Roberte as another person, owing to the fact that Roberte's spirit, actualizing itself in the intention of this other, rejects Roberte into creatable existence. Which comes around to saying that if it is through increate intellect that Roberte senses herself the object of another's intention, it is, on the other hand, in another that Roberte has the experience of increate intellect; an experience whereof a banal happening of ordinary chance like the Ascona incident is a mere counterfeit. You see that through this very operation Roberte lays herself bare and the lock to her identity is forced: displaced out of Roberte's subjective being, her consciousness immediately proposes itself as object to any other suppositum in whom increate intellect can be defined; to whom else if not to a consciousness, fascinated, I might venture to say, by this impalpable spectacle of increate intellect being exhibited in an essence again become creatable; as fascinated as Roberte herself is by this irruption of the increate into her own hitherto closed essence. Now, beginning with him in whom existence and the increate merge as one, all the way to the creatures which lack inherent existence, there is an echeloning of consciousness in which increate intellect is explicit along a scale rising from irrational unrestraint, which signifies our destruction, to rational restraint which enables us to withstand the violence of the irrational, even when we are carried away and animated by it. And if it is through an act of increate intellect that Roberte disactualizes herself *qua* Roberte to attain consciousness of another actuality which eludes us, this intellectual act coincides with one of her consciousnesses whose remove from existence, broadening, lessens their distance from the increate. A twofold attraction is immediately exerted; which of the two consciousnesses plays with respect to the other the role of existence aspiring to essence or of essence aspiring to existence, this can hardly be ascertained save through analogy with this picture, this "candid shot," which is nothing else than the simulacrum of the operation I have been discussing. An image in itself has no being; reciprocally, it is intellection through and through: the skirt burns, the body appears to be safe, but it is in fact the spirit that is burning in this body which Victor, ostensibly in order to save it, is exhibiting. . . .

ANTOINE

Victor, that's his name?

OCTAVE

Or rather Vittorio, Conte della Santa-Sede, your next tutor. He arrives tomorrow.

ANTOINE

I must ask him to give me an account of this accident.

OCTAVE

You will do better to keep still and finally realize that the question here is of an incident whose secret we are keeping to ourselves—if, that is, all this I have been saying has meant anything at all to you.

ANTOINE
(*glancing again at the scene*)

The more I look at it the less I can make out accident from incident.

OCTAVE

It could have occurred before I took the picture and elsewhere than in Victor's presence. As it happened, Santa-Sede was sitting in the front row of the audience; I knew Roberte had no particular liking for him. And so it is odd that as I get ready to photograph her, as she is used to seeing me do, this should be the very moment for her skirt to catch fire and for her to choose Vittorio. . . .

ANTOINE

She had no opportunity to choose him: he rushed spontaneously to her aid.

OCTAVE

Must one believe that your aunt's influence upon you is such that at the mere sight of her image you forget the Roberte in her? A simple accident you may call it, but something very different is contained in the photograph. I might add that in other prints from the same negative there is no sign of any fire: all that remains, but in a much more striking manner, is this extraordinary tangle of arms and legs.

ANTOINE

. . . Roberte's raised hand, seized by Vittorio . . . Show me that again, Uncle Octave, I'm sure you make your prints according to your whims. . . .

OCTAVE

You've already seen more than enough. Come along, it's late. Let's go to sleep.

II
ROBERTE CE SOIR

Emerging from the Censorship Council headquarters after the meeting she had called for the purpose of banning Octave's ignoble work, Roberte had had some trouble shaking off the giant Guardsman who, clinking his spurs, had followed her from the rue Royale; she did not finally reach home until about two in the morning. Taking the backstairs in order to avoid Octave, she enters the apartment by a secret door and slips into her dressing room, a place of sufficient size to serve for occasional work. She removes her coat, goes toward the desk on the side opposite the bathtub; this desk is simply a vanity table surmounted by a mirror, and upon its marble top she unzips her leather brief case, bulging with manuscripts awaiting her seal of approval. She sorts through its contents, fails to find Octave's work which, through some unpardonable inadvertence, she must have left behind at the office; annoyed, she gets to her feet, notices herself in the glass, her heightened color, touches her fingers to her cheek, and, her mind elsewhere, applies some lipstick to her lips. One might think her on the point of going out again, to see her tall slender form bent that way toward the mirror, her face aglow beneath the dark hair done up in thick braids, the lipstick held between her tapered fingers, her clear nails straying along the edge of her arched lips, now and then putting a fingertip to her long lashes, like all her regular features her gray eyes remaining grave despite the faint smile that appeared a moment ago when, unbuttoning her black blouse with the white cuffs, she glided a hand under her armpit. Tempted to take a bath, she retreats from the mirror where her face, once again severe, dissolves into a blur, but here in front of the toilet, next to the tub, she slides her fingers down her flanks to lift her long black skirt, when she spies, spilling from the toilet paper dispenser, some of Octave's censored work, leaves from the chapter entitled "Tacita, the Giant Guardsman and the Hunchback." Settled on the seat, for the hundredth time she rereads these lucubrations which vex her, doubtless satisfied enough with the decision she has just reached at the Council to begin to piss, albeit more furious than satisfied to not stop urinating when without a sound the door suddenly opens before the enormous personage. The crested helmet gleams not more brightly than the enamel of the teeth and the whites of the eyes in Victor's swarthy face. Beneath the broad cape flung negligently back of his epaulettes he stands there, squeezing the riding crop in his white-gloved fist while the other, posed on his hip, seems to indicate that it is from all eternity he has been holding himself so, codpiece askew and yielding passage to the tremendous member whose smooth and admirably rounded knob is trained at Roberte. Before this triumphal and insolent immobility, letting fall the pages—with that same hand, authoritative of gesture when, three hours earlier, the blue pencil between the tips of her supple fingers, Roberte had drawn her colleagues' attention to the inadmissible passages in Octave's book—she presently attempts that same gesture, the palm lightly lifted against the unbearable vision; but her face flushes and it is only barely if she succeeds in pointing imperatively with the index finger of that faltering hand: "Get out!" she believes she hears herself say in a pale voice, whereas all she does is urinate the harder. "Only what is out is visible," is the reply she gets from no perceptible voice. And, glancing at the door, it looks as though it had never been opened.

Roberte washes, readjusts her corset, then her long black skirt, striving to find calm in these reliably everyday gestures; so strong has been the intruding image that a curious disappointment suspends her agitation when she verifies that the door has remained bolted while emotion has raised the tingling warmth in her limbs to an almost fever pitch, and as she is at a loss to know what to do with it and despite herself has felt it delicious, Roberte is more than irked when at her feet she notices the riding crop, stoops to pick it up and at the instant she straightens, feels an ill-defined but heavy mass wedge underneath her skirt and hang at her calves. If Roberte at once tries to back off, her ankles gripped in a vise; to bend backward is the best she can do, and must press her knees upon invisible shoulders while from below her skirt there is uttered:

"What is to be made of the fact that something rather than nothing exists? This existence which permits things to exist which are still only in being, must it not be conceived in its own terms, independently of those things?"

Jerking up her skirt, Roberte discovers a strange hunchback, misshapen and misbegotten, with the head of a spaniel, greasy locks, and bulging blue eyes that are considering her thoughtfully. Ashamed at recognizing "The Preacher," her best Council informer, and furious at her shame, Roberte aims a first cut of the riding crop at him as he ducks under her skirt again, from where he continues:

"Be it conceived in itself or be it not, there is no being rid of it, of itself it constantly returns, and if there is something which makes existence be existence, in that something you have its essence." (*Words which, coming from inside her skirt, Roberte only confusedly makes out, for to dodge the blow that landed on his neck, the Hunchback has burrowed his face between Roberte's thighs and it is with his nose pressed to the Inspectress' underpanties he continues:*) "Now as of the moment it is this which permits or does not permit to exist, which permits or does not permit to name, would one have the right to name it censorship as if from the beginning there had always been censorship? For the fact one cannot any longer name it God can hardly be otherwise explained than by something in existence which henceforth forbids that it be named God."

Down comes a second blow, deadened by Roberte's own skirt which she raises to discover him again: it is with a strange smile that the Hunchback gazes at her, her arm lifted high, fingers shining on the leather handle of the crop brandished above the rich braids of hair that frame a face gone scarlet, dilated nostrils fluttering from indignation, when, upon the point of striking a third time, Roberte feels her wrist seized; taking her from behind, the Guardsman's gauntlet sweeps slantwise, rips through her black blouse, moves downward grazing Roberte's chest, splits her brassiere and lands squarely upon her breast, leaving her shoulder bare. At the very first bite Roberte lets go of the whip while her other breast tumbles through the tear in her blouse, beginning with a pink nipple popping through a curtain of black silk.

THE GUARDSMAN
(*fondling Roberte's breasts*)

Forgive us these developments, Madame, we others who are but simple substances, produced without the flesh wherewith here you are so agreeably clad, you who enjoy a dual nature. But we others, by an instant's reversal of the living thought we were, we subsist—for what is to be done with our being—dead thoughts without any chance of returning to our former state. Were you nothing but a pure spirit, as sometimes you feign to be at the Censorship Council, you would be no less incessantly assailed by thoughts more enormous still than these you are indulging in this evening. For if this flesh was given you as they say out of mercy to be your defense against our visitation, who else summoned us this evening if not you yourself who gazed at that mirror and who have little belief in that mercy? Who else if not you standing before that mirror, posing for a pure spirit with such perfection that we believed we saw ourselves in your gestures? But as nothing more was involved than the simulacrum of your soul created to inhabit this body which thanks to us has been able to transport you this evening, see yourself still free to choose between an existence enslaved to the spirits in which you have no belief and the life of the flesh which is the issue of the ways of a God in whom you are hardly more wont to believe. Is this not the first proper name you suppressed in your contemporaries' vocabulary? And having done so, what are you going to do with us, and what are we going to do with your flesh? Shall we be sparing of it because it is yet capable of speaking, or else shall we treat it as if it were to keep silence forever?

While he fixes her hand which has just released the whip, the Inspectress thinks to move the other to the gauntlet fondling her breasts; thus to see them become the object of a separate intelligence, it seems to Roberte she is feeling them for the first time, never has she seen them so docile nor their nipples swell and harden so readily as in the hollow of the

broad gauntlet which is massaging them. But as if still un-
willing to bow to the evidence, she tenses her hand anew and
lifts it to have it seized at the wrist; and as he wishes to draw
this hand to his mouth, that mouth Roberte dares neither
dwell upon nor notice in the mirror any more than she dares
look at herself there, keeping her eyes lowered she closes
the captive hand; but so cunning are the bites applied to her
neck that she unbends her fingers, spreads them, baring their
soft underside and the base of her thumb to which he so
skillfully puts his teeth that she is shaken from head to toe.

The Guardsman

We ask no more, it is enough for us to visit dual substances to convince them that with us there is no need for
any such tawdry relics. (*Stabbing his tongue into Roberte's
palm, he lifts her wedding ring and slides it up from the
bottom to the top of her ring finger, then down, then up
again, secret of a game whose efficacity he seems to understand; Roberte would like to free her hand, but he goes on:*)
Octavo? Pro isto elucubrante, why these grimaces, why this
fuss? These charming fingers you clench in vain, this ring
finger so conductible to the lifeless cogitations that from the
tip of this fingernail in ictu we convey to your utrumsit, do
they not prove, these fingers, that you cling still to your
fleshly envelope the while we believe we have it already in
our power? If it is true that it is to be reborn from out of its
dust, speak, Madame, speak, unclamp those so well-painted
lips, that mouth so well-made to open that had there been a
mouth given to me, I would crush yours with kisses from fear
lest it name us too soon. Convinced at least of your flesh,
we'd be quits, and discharged, though sadly so, from what remains to be done this evening. It is rather to deny it that this
silence invites us. Consequently: Andiamo!

And as Roberte, now held by both wrists, strains in a futile effort to pull free and manages only to jerk her hand loose, the Guardsman snatches the ring from her finger, and continues:

Your great sin in our eyes, Madame, is that you serve two masters, believing in one only so far as that belief is useful to you in disserving to the other, truthfully believing in neither of them. In relation to us, you attempt to maintain the fraudulent doctrine of dual substance. Are we the undesirable thoughts of your mind, then to us you oppose the muteness of a flesh to be withheld from our operations; why withheld, if you please, since by opposing it to your thoughts, tonight, which are nowhere else than in your spirit, it is from your very spirit you divorce this flesh; what now becomes of its integrity if it is not found in the principle of the resurrection of bodies? But in forbidding your poets, your artists, your players to describe, to paint, and above all to enact what we are operating upon you at the present moment, upon them you impose the muteness of integral flesh as if it were already the pure silence of spirits. Thus in relation to these composite substances, to these dual natures who employ speech to denounce their own duplicity, you have the nerve to act as a simple substance, that of the spirits who for lack of what is called passible flesh must be without hope of redemption and subsist valiantly in a spiritual death such as ours which you deny the instant you oppose to us the appearance of a flesh, as if it could be reborn incorruptible. Might you then be in agreement with us who refute this so-called mystery as a slur upon our dignity? Not a bit of it. For if a simple substance's pure silence is due to the absence of a speaking flesh, you clumsily confuse this silence with the muteness of a living flesh. Now the muteness of a double substance, which only exists because this double substance lives outside of being, agitates the spirit which subsists upon its own death. And the substance composed of a soul and a body which thus pretends to simulate the death of a spiritual substance provokes aggression from the being wherein at our death we subsist. (*To the Hunchback:*) Piatto!

At these words, the Hunchback at her feet gives a tug at her skirt and off it comes. Skirtless, Roberte's immediate reaction is to raise her knee and with the intent of fending off the spy with her heel, she plants her shoe on the Hunchback's forehead who, wrapping his arms around her shins, once again clasps her long legs and, his nostrils tickling Roberte's thighs, snuffles from her garter snaps upward to the seams of her corset still rich with a treasure tightly confined behind a triangular yoke of mesh ensconced in her crotch whence dance no more than one or two stray wisps of her bush, but whence there now also comes forth the Inspectress' embarrassment in all its warmth, while to animal odor there is added the scent of her freed hand which she claps straight to the vee underneath her corset.

THE GUARDSMAN

God forbid, Madame, that we call into question your aptness for simple substantiality; for if you act like a simple substance and deal with none but other simple substances, not only in keeping silent, but in obliging others to keep silent over the various counterfeitings of the spirit by the flesh, it will no longer do for you to deny the resurrection of bodies, to ban Vatican propaganda on the one hand, and to deprive pornographers of their livelihood on the other, you have yet to give us guarantees and consent to abide loyally by the inexorable law governing the communication between pure spirits; with more logic than plausibility the

Vaticanists suppose that among us it is not the spirit which is modified upon receiving what another spirit gives it to understand, but this other who makes known to it what he wishes to designate. Now, they say, if we are well acquainted with all innate forms, perfection for us would consist in knowledge of the particular just as it would consist for you, Madame, in the abstraction of all things. How now can any exchange be established between you and us; come to the abstraction of yourself, what would you have to designate to us that we did not know already unless it were your proper will? To be sure, this will must escape us if there is only the author hiding its secret from us; but as of the moment you deny its repository, how could this will have anything secret for us when already, if unable to seize the will itself, we can, inversely at least, seize it through its objects? For, in as much as we are your separate thoughts, we know more of the nature of what it is astir in you than can you, and are better able than you to interpret the signs, however equivocal they may be, through which you might hope to mislead us. (*To the Hunchback*:) Piatto!

Thereupon the Hunchback, hanging onto Roberte's corset, gives it such a yank it splits clean down the front, denuding the Inspectress' flanks and belly; and Roberte's bush, hitherto tight-packed in her crotch behind the netting, unfurls all its hairy abundance while the acrid odor steams up from her utrumsit. And as The Preacher, boldly putting forth his tongue, sets sedulously to straightening out the tufts of Roberte's garden, the Inspectress shoots her lithe fingers into the thicket where amidst the darkness her nails twinkle as they come together or scatter, chasing the Hunchback's tongue, trying to head off its sallies. For if the back of that hand disputes his entry there for the safeguarding of principles affirmed three hours before, the already humid palm ascertains their vanity, already the accomplice of fingers which steal farther forward than they ought.

THE GUARDSMAN

Wishing to secure the life of the spirit against spiritual death, our author created the dual substance wherein spirit became bound up with a shadowy region, this flesh, image of the secrecy which all created will shares with him. But we laid bare this treason in our regard by putting into the flesh corruption by the spirit, which is nothing but a quest after the knowledge of signs. Then he, the simplest and most secret of natures, he goes and makes himself double in nature, and occupies this dark region to become himself its sign, indecipherable to us, and permits you others to survive our indiscretion; but whoever joins us in rejecting this indecipherable sign as a mystification, instead of worshiping it as a mystery, knows full well that the Word is nothing but an incarnation of betrayal and the workings of the flesh the pantomime of spirits. But what are you driving at, Madame? With one hand you persecute the Vatican scribes, with the other you suppress the writings of the pornographers. No resurrection of the flesh, you say to the former, and that is very fine. But what is the use of prohibiting the latter from repeating this truth in our mimic style? No redemption of the spirit by perishable flesh, certainly; but why then do you defend it as an inviolable silence? You are not for pantomime? And if you dislike pantomime, why the devil do you silence the actors?

Ridded of her girdle, but her right hand a prisoner in the Guardsman's fist, never had Roberte found herself so over-

whelmed by this body of hers to defend, by all these retreats
to cover, by so many salients to screen, for which her still
free hand could not suffice, when in between the buttocks of
the Inspectress the Guardsman's knee was already nudging
itself and all down her thighs she feels the leather of the
boots, to the back of her sagging knees. Although tall herself,
Roberte begins to appreciate her aggressor's monumental
stature; pinning her with an arm thrown around her midriff,
he presses her hard against the frogs and loops or the bedizen-
ments on a jacket which she makes out running the whole
length of her own back as a shiver travels from her nape
downward to the base of her spine and farther still. It is here,
well above her flanks, where the buckle is digging in, and
here the swordbelt would be; a still unfastened swordbelt,
and Roberte feels that her own fingers might already be
helping to unfasten it in order to move past to something a
little lower down; but lower down, nothing precise, that
nothing precise which like a flame darts near to dart immediately away again; the less there is something there where there
ought to be a peremptory arrival, the more Roberte's expectation sears the contour of her own behind; seized by a dizziness and by this dizziness as if endowed with foul sight, she
sees them, her own buttocks, tense and agape where they are
cleft, as before her very eyes the gauntlet goes on harrying
the nipples of her breasts which stab wildly into emptiness,
and as the foreign attention which has roused them to a
stand routs what is left of will in the arm lolling languidly
upon her belly, its elbow upon her navel, its hand over her
bush, that slender hand which is containing her utrumsit has
ceased to heed her anymore by the time the Guardsman calls
upon her:

If you wish us to keep silent over what we are in the midst

of doing, disavow your body, own to the existence of the pure spirit. If we be evocable, your body is yet revocable. How else would it be so delicious if not in virtue of the Word it hides: express it then, unless you would have the irrevocable brought about. Banish these thoughts, speak, and we disappear. You are still? Let us act.

With a powerful upward thrust forcing his knee between her buttocks he makes her thighs open wide; Roberte's fingers loosen upon her utrumsit, all its volutes are shaken in front of the Hunchback's face. More, she even puts out her hand to cover the mouth of this Council informer, and it pleases Octave to have the dwarf see the Inspectress' raised palm, not so long ago slapped dryly down upon the words for outlawing, presently damp and moistened by her own cogitation, the clear lacquer on her fingernails already dulled by an unnamable unction; another lick given by the Hunchback's tongue to that palm slick with deceit and Roberte will herself see the way through her bush open to her own flagitation; is it the Hunchback's tongue struggling there, no, it is her own impertinence which emerges in spurts: quick as a flash, the gauntlet, parting the fleece overgrowing Roberte's utrumsit, wide and deep, entirely liberates the Inspectress' quidest; and as she would yet put a covering hand to this attribute of her taciturn arrogance, of unsuspected size, the Guardsman deftly nips the quidest which erects prodigiously between the aggressor's leather thumb and forefinger.

THE GUARDSMAN

This outburst of merriment on your part, Madame, vexes us; capable of speaking, you say nothing, and pretending to be silent, you snigger. . . . Is that the truth you laid such solemn store by, this your flesh now pronounces, or is there another in this obscure place where we are going to go to search for it?

Does she think to hide from her spy's sight that which she still disavows, lifting her knee; the Hunchback steps through between her thighs, clutches the full curves of her buttocks, pats them, comforts them; finally spreads them.

THE GUARDSMAN
Learn, Madame, that the shadow of a doubt, such as it would be cast in you by a way of thinking more enriched by love of silence than can be yours by hatred of eloquence, could finally lead nowhere else than to your refutation, while here it is that in this fraudulent flesh you share with us the fate of simple substances subsisting at their death. . . .

At these words, Roberte does not know if it is from shame she trembles because the sentence is carried out, enormous, impetuous, scalding, between her buttocks, or whether it is from pleasure she is sweating, because this sentence does wide violence to her vacuum; but while the sedcontra penetrates the Inspectress to the point of confounding within her the stiffness of the acquittal and the elasticity of the penalty, Roberte has been unable to anticipate the gesture of the gauntlet which upon the Inspectress' quidest, in monstrous erection, slips the ring it has just plucked off her finger; in so doing the sedcontra withdraws from the vacuum, from where Roberte looses three farts.

THE GUARDSMAN
Besides, if the flesh is nothing but a lure, speech is nothing but wind; it is hence of the spirit.

Then seizing Roberte's fingers, he obliges her to put her own quidest in the most perfect state; in such a way that ringed, reared in all its oily sauciness, this latter is promptly mouthed by the Hunchback; to such good purpose that the Inspectress, unable to contain herself any longer, washes her spy's gullet with her wickedness. . . .

INTERLUDE

Roberte, it must be recognized, limits Roberte for the same reason the Roberte I represent to myself this evening is limited by the circumstances of the aggression she has just undergone, just as are these circumstances from the viewpoint of all that could contribute to making this a still more perfect aggression.

While Dacquin takes me to task for my spirit's impatience before indeterminate Roberte which renders it unable to recognize, at least, that her nature does not in itself imply any determination whether by the expectation of an aggression in her (the reverse side of my impatience), or by the aggressor or by my own representation—although she could become the object of the one or the other; Hochheim, for his part, is more particularly worried by the insinuating conjunctive locution in my mind: this *although,* and is preoccupied by my transition into the subjunctive, from indeterminate Roberte to her determination by a compound of form and matter thanks to which she would be unable to escape the most venturesome; a transition no sooner accomplished than it turns into insatiable reference of Roberte, surrendered to Victor, to Roberte whom I continue to represent to myself and who herself perpetually surrenders and refers herself to my most venturesome curiosity. There, in effect, Roberte betrays her dissimilarity within the framework of her similarity to my absolute curiosity. All subsisting created form possessing being and not being its being—as they put it—it is necessary that the Roberte I represented to myself receive this representation of this evening and, consequently, be reduced to within the limits of a certain nature, if Dacquin is to be credited. It is therefore not surprising that Hochheim, concerned over my state, speaks to me first of all of Roberte's fitness for representation, of Roberte as posing a subject: this evening's Roberte in her attitude of a woman waiting to be surprised by a desirable intruder; and that next he affirms that it is the Roberte susceptible of representation which confers its reality upon Roberte assailed tonight.

Now Hochheim's little trick—in which he sees a method that would be salutary for my spirit—is to distinguish two sorts of causes behind the actuality of Roberte this evening, one which he says is final, Victor, who enables Roberte to get herself assailed this evening (without however having fore-seen any Victor), and a formal cause, my curiosity, which supplies what in his jargon Hochheim calls the quiddity of her existence (in the circumstances, the surprise of Roberte waiting to be surprised by Victor). One might interject here that before Dacquin's indeterminate Roberte is informed— as they say—as Roberte awaiting assault and at the same time being surprised at being assailed by Victor, she is found, since my curiosity has already specified her as Roberte having to wait to be assaulted, in a still relative determination in rela- tion to Roberte herself waiting to be assailed in the evening and, the evening having come, surprised at it having been by Victor. There is by consequence a limitation of Roberte brought about at the very instant Roberte assaulted by Victor is actual for me. Now Hochheim, we remember, said that it is the formal cause—my curiosity—that would confer to Roberte the quiddity of her existence. Form, in Hochheim's language, is limitless perfection in the sense that it strives to be the perfection of perfections, in the very same way the circumstances of tonight's scene (the matter, they say) bestow its definite character to the form of my curiosity; thus, Roberte who is awaiting assault receives her own limitations from Roberte assaulted.

My impatience in the face of her indeterminate character, my curiosity which confuses this impatience with Roberte's very waiting, my curiosity, I say, for having wished to express itself as perfection of perfections in Roberte awaiting assault, would then have drawn up short of the mark as of the instant it became concern for perfection and through this concern, turning Roberte's waiting into her surprise, brought her actuality to pass only accompanied by its limitation; for if my curiosity were thus to have conferred her quiddity to Roberte waiting to be surprised, the final cause demanded in advance that Victor assail her tonight as he did. Now, just as tonight's circumstances, after they have occurred, are still aspiring to the form they have in rry curiosity, so the infinite variations they ruled out, in occuring as they did, aspire to even more actuality. An immediately limited actuality, points out Hochheim, who would like to see me suspended in this aspiration. No doubt I share with him what he calls the tension between the form and its actuality; between the Roberte destined to be assaulted and my representation of the Roberte who is waiting to be—once again, I myself will add. But as his mind hovers in regions far above the cloaca wherein mine wallows, he hence sees nothing therein but a pure and simple degradation, by my spirit, of the tension between the creature and the increate being of all things, between that which is *hors de sa cause* and the cause itself.

III

WHERE WHAT WAS TO BE DEMONSTRATED IS ADVANCED

At the home of Octave and Roberte,
in the living room, late afternoon.
Roberte, Octave, Antoine.

ROBERTE

You could at least have asked my opinion before taking on your Victor as Antoine's tutor.

OCTAVE

More recriminations? It seemed to me I had your tacit agreement.

ROBERTE

Tacit! What shabby insincerity!

OCTAVE

What is the use of going into the discussion again? You did, didn't you, leave me completely free to act upon this subject as I saw fit? Besides, Antoine is old enough to give us an opinion of his own and for it to carry some weight. He gets on wonderfully with Victor.

ROBERTE

Oh, I don't doubt it! This Victor will be able to tell him all sorts of thrilling tales: his adventures at the Vatican, or among the war criminals, or among the fashion designers. . . .

OCTAVE

What kind of nonsense are you telling me now? The
Vatican, war criminals, fashion designers . . .

ROBERTE

You perfectly well understand what those substantives
mean.

OCTAVE

My poor dear, you mix everything up, and you do it
deliberately.

ROBERTE

Not at all. To the contrary, I have a very clear view of
the marvelous mixture of ingredients that make up your
orthodoxy. And now Victor to top it all off: officer in the
Pontifical Guard, dancing master . . .

OCTAVE

In all this is there anything I am to make out apart from
the prejudice you have against the Pontifical Guard or some
grudge against the reconverted dancing master?

ROBERTE

Don't try to sidetrack the conversation. He's just the right
person, isn't he, this disoriented individual full of inferiority
complexes and all the arrogance that's usually there by way
of compensation, this model of a disturbed mind, this hatchet
man of degenerate obscurantism, to guide a high-strung child
like Antoine?

OCTAVE

Come now, my dear, admit that all that's untrue, all the
more untrue because the necessities of the Church elude you:

part of its mission is to be all things to all men: in a world
as convulsed by upheavals as ours, prone to such unpredictable metamorphoses, it has got to have supple agents. . . .

ROBERTE

Supple agents, my poor Octave, you hit the nail on the
head. Supple agents capable of unpredictable metamorphoses,
let's say a word or two about them: your Holy See parachutist who has just landed here as your nephew's tutor!
But what else could one expect from an apologist for international fraud of your stripe. . . .

OCTAVE

I was expecting this broadside. Well now: what are they
up to, this Holy See parachutist and this apologist, as you
describe me, for international fraud?

ROBERTE

. . . the shady operation that consists in passing the
atheist off for a pervert, and the perverse atheist for a masked
Christian . . .

OCTAVE

Whatever are you talking about?

ROBERTE

From whom then did Antoine get that book he was reading only last night? From you, or has Victor already been
giving him such things? The mere title alone is enough to
make one ill: *Sade mon prochain*!

OCTAVE

Make who ill?

ROBERTE

Any self-respecting atheist. As for your Sade, you can have him for all of me. But what a means to use to try to convince us that one cannot be an atheist without automatically being perverted! Perverse, you insult God to make Him exist, therefore you believe in Him, that proves you secretly worship Him! A scheme by which you think you can disgust the believer out of his healthy conviction; an easy operation, to be sure, since every sick spirit has always been ripe for Christianism—or cretinism, that would be a better way of putting it.

OCTAVE

Hush!

ROBERTE

I intend to have my say, or else I denounce your parachutist!

OCTAVE

It's bound to amount to the same thing. Well, go ahead then. Tell me, what does this "I denounce your parachutist" mean?

ROBERTE

One thing alone matters to me, and it is to preserve Antoine's still intact common sense. But what are you doing? You throw him into the arms of this degenerate aristocrat who, to begin with, resigned from the Pontifical Guard . . .

OCTAVE

I would have thought you'd score that to his credit. . . .

ROBERTE

. . . in connection with some scandal or other involving gambling or corruption of minors; who goes off to be the lounge-lizard at an American woman tourist's place on Capri; who when the Reich occupies Rome appears as Fascist liaison officer attached to Nazi headquarters, then as secret agent whose job is to keep an eye on the Vatican; who suddenly vanishes and is not heard of again until he turns up in the affair of the camp of Communist hostages. . . .

OCTAVE

The camp of hostages affair? Listen carefully, Antoine!

ROBERTE

There, a bare few hours before the liberation of Rome, the poor wretches who have been kept for months penned up in a quarry, see a parachutist drop out of the sky and land holding a monstrance. . . .

OCTAVE

It's too beautiful to be true. . . .

ROBERTE

It's appalling and it's true. . . .

OCTAVE

Hence true because appalling. . . .

ROBERTE

Probably, and what happens? Some, in their distress, fall upon their knees, others think it's a trap, a fight starts and the Fascist militia shoots into the heap. What is behind all this?

Why, a bet between the Nazi commandant and the parachutist, alleges the latter who is none other than your Vittorio della Santa-Sede. If I show the Host to your hostages, all of them, Communists or not, will adore it—so he claims he said to Binsnicht, the Nazi in charge of the camp who, for his part, so the story went, agreed to free the hostages and turn himself in as a prisoner if Santa-Sede won.

OCTAVE
At what moment could they have made such a wager?

ROBERTE
The fact remains that a few minutes later the hostage camp, transformed into a charnel house, is liberated by the Allies; together with the Nazi commandant, Vittorio is arrested as an accomplice or instigator and, of course, is disavowed by the Vatican. Both are incarcerated in a fortress; Victor is shortly released. He keeps in contact with Binsnicht, who is to be tried as a war criminal and entrusts personal documents to him; but a year after the end of hostilities, Anglo-Saxon justice dismisses Binsnicht's case on grounds of insufficient evidence; he thinks it wisest to change identity and makes a deal with Santa-Sede: they swap names and papers. Binsnicht has told Vittorio that he has a rendezvous in Switzerland with an Argentine industrialist, an adept of Nazism and who arranges passage to Argentina for any Nazi who is in difficulty. This Argentine knows Binsnicht will present himself under Vittorio's name. But no sooner does he set foot in Milan than the German is spotted in the street by a survivor from the camp, who, instead of notifying the police, stirs up the mob; Binsnicht is massacred. Meanwhile, Vittorio has taken it into his head that he can get away with playing the role of

Binsnicht. He goes to Switzerland, finds the Argentine, who does not know Binsnicht by face or that the German has been lynched; he simply expects to have him come under the name of Vittorio. Greeting Santa-Sede, he imagines that the man in front of him is Binsnicht.

OCTAVE

Vittorio thus passes off his true identity for the false identity of somebody else. Antoine, I ask you to take note of this detail: Vittorio is said to have sought to incarnate a war criminal.

ROBERTE

It was simply a question of exploiting Binsnicht's documents which Vittorio had used to concoct some imaginary memoirs; the Argentine was to buy them for a considerable price.

OCTAVE

Look here! You actually saw these memoirs with your own eyes?

ROBERTE

But now it comes out in the newspapers: some American officers have identified the lynched Binsnicht as Binsnicht. About to be sued for fraud and imposture, Victor goes and hides himself—where? In a Benedictine monastery; and as he confides in the prior, the prior has one of his monks sent for; it is Binsnicht in person who, far from having been killed at Milan, has done nothing else than precede Vittorio into this high place, under the name of Vittorio. Which of the two is Santa-Sede, which is Binsnicht? If anybody knows it ought to be the prior. Nevertheless, after another eclipse Vittorio is found associated, this time, with a Paris fashion designer, with whom he falls out after having accepted an order for a set of costumes for a ballet that never took place.

OCTAVE

A ballet that never took place! If all of your picture is exact, you have to admit that the whole thing is brilliant.

ANTOINE

Fascinating, Aunt Roberte!

OCTAVE

The only thing that surprises me is that it be you who tell us all this, that it be precisely you who give us these details. However, you pass over a later incarnation. . . .

ROBERTE

Which one?

OCTAVE

Vittorio, steward to Madame de Watteville at Ascona.

ROBERTE

To Madame de Watteville at Ascona?

OCTAVE

And you neglect to speak of one particular . . . which concerns you. . . .

ROBERTE

Concerns me?

OCTAVE

The fact that he saved you from the fire at Madame de Watteville's.

ROBERTE

Saved me from the fire . . . What! It was he?

OCTAVE

He himself, my dear, the "war criminal." You ought to have been the first to know it.

ROBERTE

You concealed his name from me—it's shameful! You knew all about it all the time!

OCTAVE

To be sure—but I had no way of foreseeing your maneuvers in front of the fireplace and of warning you the moment before it happened.

ROBERTE

My maneuvers! What are you implying? Your nephew must . . .

OCTAVE

Antoine is too grateful to him for that chivalrous gesture—as indeed he is for yours.

ROBERTE
(*breathless*)

For mine?

ANTOINE

All human respect, Aunt Roberte, was abolished by the Cross.

ROBERTE

What are you saying? You too, are you beginning to disguise pure insolence in false blasphemies?

OCTAVE

Antoine, you are to have a "war criminal" for a tutor!

ANTOINE

I am neither blaspheming nor being insolent, Aunt Roberte. From Christ onward, no human morality holds together anymore.

ROBERTE

And so the Son of God died to enable you to outrage your fellow man all the better!

ANTOINE

God had to allow His only Son to be killed in order that it be remembered ever afterward that no human law can ever restrain men from killing other men.

ROBERTE
(*quieting down, caressing Antoine*)

Don't you understand that it was against just such arguments your Christ spoke? And has He not been shamelessly turned into a spokesman for what He wished to destroy? The idea of a god who would assure the impunity of crime by surrendering His Son to the executioner? Do you not see that Christ was the first of the godless? Showing how one ought to live in kindness, because no God commands any such thing, in justice, because no God rewards it, in truth, because no God reveals it; for what does saying "God alone is good" amount to if not that the mere idea of God dispenses humans from being good and just and truthful? Is it not on purpose that He is made to say that no one could follow Him unless he took on His Cross? Was that not to have Him play the part of the Son sacrificed by the Father, this Father who is nothing else than fate reconciled, or not? In fact, the only miracle I find in the story of His life is that He, the enemy of the priests and of their god, He, the first of the atheists, He was made into the Son of the monstrous idol He spurned beneath His feet during the short while He lived on earth. He, the comforter of the poor, they twist His words: you shall always have the poor among you, but you shall not always have Me—that is, to remind you that you shall always have the poor—and He is turned into the single poor man, and no more thought is given to the masses of the poor. There are scarcely more than two or three of His sayings which I am prepared to consider authentic: Man was not made for the sake of the Sabbath, but the Sabbath for man. Love thine enemies. Bless them who hate thee. And there is the saying that may perhaps be the key to all the others He really did pronounce, to all His acts: Judge not if ye would not yourselves be judged as ye have judged others. Thus, there is never any other judge than the one we institute ourselves. Nothing so well disproves the existence of an eternal Judge and nothing has been so fraudulent as to ascribe prophecies of a Last Judgment to Him, unless this judgment, if it is to be the last, be the sum of the consequences that will result from this terrible infirmity in us which makes us seek a sinner, and if the innocent has already expiated the latter's guilt, what is the use of a further judgment? Now, this lack of an eternal judge and the resultant impossibility to judge, they make up the sole truth with which He identified Himself: the absence of truth. Whence the necessity to love even our enemies, to turn the other cheek to insult, to accept everything without murmur—happiness or misfortune. Whence, above all, the impossibility of conceding an immortal soul—as if, granted this immortality, we could work ill upon our neighbor or heap blessings upon him, weigh his merits and allot him happiness or miseries proportional to immortality! A fine way to console one's self for the evils or irreparable wrongs suffered by those unlucky ones beyond number who desired nothing more than an end to their existence! Indeed! There has got to be a resurrection of the flesh, not only for the vision of the beatitude of some, but for the sight of the others enduring everlasting hellfire. What more atrocious picture than this one they show us of the meek and mild Saviour reawakening the dead in order to make them suffer forever! What common measure can there be between eternity, if there is one, the notion of which conjures up such gloom and horror, and the instant during which a mistake, a crime is unthinkingly committed, when it has been said to us: Judge not!

OCTAVE

For the reason that immortal souls can produce only equally unending actions, none of our deeds, none of our thoughts can ever be abolished; not even the words you are uttering now.

ROBERTE
(*putting an arm around Antoine, who gazes in rapture
at his aunt's hand lying upon his shoulder*)
I should like to have Antoine realize that nothing would

be of any value in this world were we not to accept that our life ends in certain nothingness—nothing would concern us, not even the possibility of an eternal life. But let's say that this eternity were granted us; to this I answer with the saying which is perhaps the essential thing in the pure atheistic doctrine: charity does not seek to be rewarded. Little then does it matter to charity, to perish or to never perish, little does it matter, everlasting torments or the sight of bliss. . . .

ANTOINE
But charity is nothing other than God Himself!

ROBERTE
. . . Little does it matter to charity, I say to you, that you name it God if you dare do so, this god who encourages men to licentiousness after having forbidden them to be licentious under the pretense that the blood of his son has expiated everything in advance, and that all one need do is believe in him—into the confessional with you and everything will be forgotten. But if you want my opinion on this Christ of yours, who for that matter does not care in the least whether I take him seriously or not, once he is this charity—which is the only lesson we can draw from the saying: Love thine enemies—we cannot even know who our fellow man is, since we are called upon to abstain from all judgment.

OCTAVE
If it is not an eternal and therefore immutable judge above us who admonished us not to turn judges ourselves, and if this is something beyond a statement from the oriental sage to which you reduce Jesus, it may then be, to the contrary,

that Love thine enemies is the very worst sort of advice to follow; a piece of advice you yourself have already rejected; were you not judging Victor just a moment ago?

ROBERTE

(*at a loss for what to say and blushing*)

Why, I didn't judge him . . . as one person to another . . . but in the name of . . . the name of . . .

OCTAVE

But in the name of something all the same? In the name then of what?

ROBERTE

In the name of the historical situation of our times which may be the only criterion we have left for determining with whom we are dealing, for establishing who and what we are, what we ought to avoid becoming again, what we are capable of becoming. Your Victor? Or rather the collection of odds and ends which goes by that name? Why, it is this historical product I am judging in terms of the state our society is in, a *déclassé* who subsists by slipping now into what might be called a form of recreation presently appreciated in a certain social milieu, now into another, anachronistic, which is still current in your milieu. For, after all, what would you have me think of an individual who, flitting between the Vatican and rue de la Paix poshness, feels a need to play the "war criminal"? It's simply abject.

OCTAVE

Perhaps a need to live the distress of another.

ROBERTE

Is there any greater distress than having to attribute false crimes to one's self? And is it to a man who has come to that pass you mean to entrust Antoine?

OCTAVE

And charity, Roberte, the pure essence of atheist doctrine?

ROBERTE

Are you being facetious? The charitable thing might be to teach your Victor how to work; he does work in his own way, may he succeed in it, but it is no service you render him when you put an adolescent under his care. What is he naturally cut out for? To be a walk-on, a journalist, an acrobat, a conversationalist? I have nothing to say against all that. But when he starts to theologize, then, if you don't mind, I become worried. For all I know he has something the matter with him that makes him compromise the success of whatever he happens to undertake: what is he trying to punish himself for? For having run out on the Holy See, or for being a little too good-looking? No doubt, the trouble is that he is neither superficial enough nor far enough sunk into the pit. So leave him where he is. It's probably too late anyhow, and I have no good reason for bothering over him. What else am I to say unless that we have here one of the many picturesque phenomena of the age, amusing, moving for you, I'm sure, but disquieting as soon as they are used to contribute to the education of a youngster, and who, to sum it all up, arise from this sort of psychic parasitism nowadays constituted by religion, art, and literature. There are the three monsters which keep up the contemporary obsession they live from: religion with the notion of original sin remains their great provider; art and literature are their great exploiters; and while for the time being they feign an opposition to the first, they are thick as thieves when it comes to profiting from the great attraction of the day, that of this unrealizable evil you pursue in vain and for which the image of contemporary woman has to pay the price . . . these feigned tortures . . . you inflict upon us and without which . . . it seems that the men of our times are incapable of fecondating us. . . .

OCTAVE

And what does this mean? Feigned tortures? Are they tortures or aren't they?

ROBERTE

The more so in as much as trying to make us suffer and not succeeding once and for all, you increase our sufferings through your impotence.

OCTAVE

You are doing nothing else than giving Antoine a definition of original sin. . . .

ROBERTE

A pretty paradoxical definition, with my outlook, and which couldn't please anybody but you. No, man is incapable of evil; but what incites him to cause suffering and to suffer from the fact is that he thinks he is achieving it. That is why we must destroy the remnants of this notion of a Church which leads you to believe you have achieved your goal because of us, and all this literature which fosters its legend and perpetuates its images.

OCTAVE

My dear, the Church and the art which you wish to destroy purge us of all our filth by the remembrance of death; on this side of death, all is filth, once one has got past death all is serenity beyond. Religion and art constitute all we have of dignity. . . .

ROBERTE

Yes, I know, you are dead. But why don't you live and place your dignity in not abusing the human being! For what else is the heart of the matter if not this necessity for abuse? Not having been able to eliminate this necessity from the idea of reproduction, they fabricated this idea of original sin.

OCTAVE

It is the other way around. It was in order to eliminate it . . .

ROBERTE

. . . But it's the most resounding failure! For if I cannot have children from a man except upon condition I play the victim so that he can play my victimizer, if it's only with the idea of doing evil he is able to impregnate me and if the mere idea of doing something natural renders him impotent, because of this notion of sin with which the Church brands the act of love, since the sacrament of marriage is simply a dispensation it grants him, man is still satisfying a vague craving for evil, he is ashamed to perform a natural act; so that, either way, carnal intercourse, unpardoned or pardonable, always implies the idea of evil-doing. . . .

OCTAVE

Upon this condition alone does it become an act of the spirit.

ROBERTE

I don't want anything to do with your spirit if it means sickness.

OCTAVE

Seen from the point of view of an animal, the spirit, no doubt, is a sickness; all in all, however, the plight of the faithful dog is pretty sorrowful. But for man, to confine one's self to performing natural acts is not only capitulation, it is not only boredom, it is a profound affliction; we are made for better than that, why, we are entrusted with a higher task, and if it is by virtue of the idea of evil that we can transcend our limits, blessed be this idea of evil that you take for an illusion. . . .

ROBERTE

Excuse me, my friend: insofar as I know, evil, according to your Church, is to deny what you call spiritual life. Am I right?

OCTAVE

Absolutely.

ROBERTE

And nevertheless, if it is by virtue of the idea of evil we are able to transcend ourselves, our power to deny the spirit would be a way of remaining faithful to the spirit?

OCTAVE

That is exactly it.

ROBERTE

That is exactly absurd: I who deny the spirit am all the more spiritual for doing so!

OCTAVE

Not yet, my dear, since the idea of evil has not got the virtue of carrying you outside yourself, of driving you to distraction. . . .

ROBERTE

Is there anything more revolting than to propose temptation to evil as the means for attaining to the good? And is it not precisely this that vitiates the very basis of all your detestable systems?

OCTAVE

But what else is temptation but that surging thrust of freedom which transports us out of ourselves?

ROBERTE

For you, this being transported out of one's self is nothing more than a morbid sensation you seek . . . from assaulting a person abusively. . . .

OCTAVE
(*with a hypocritically dreamy air*)
From assaulting a person . . . ?

ROBERTE

This transport that you prompt in others by dint of explaining it to them with your "mythy" dogmas. And it's just those very things we have got to destroy.

OCTAVE

Then destroy the human conscience.

ROBERTE

No, on the contrary, to cure it from your dialectical infection, that is what I am after.

OCTAVE

To end up with what?

ROBERTE

With the absence of any cause for remorse.

OCTAVE

That is to say?

ROBERTE

By doing away with temptation.

OCTAVE

Why not simply say with freedom, which amounts to extinguishing the spirit. . . .

ROBERTE

Not at all. It amounts to establishing order there.

OCTAVE

By reducing it to bondage . . .

ROBERTE

But bondage to the good.

OCTAVE

Go ahead, Roberte, secularize away, secularize the celestial order where the saints lose the capacity for evil, fixed as they forever are in the vision of Supreme Good. . . .

ROBERTE

. . . Which if it is ever to come about will only be brought about by men and for men when, having given up their freedom, from science and its disciplines they learn another use of our bodies in our relations with others. Indeed, if the nature of the spirit demands the capacity for evil, to rid ourselves of the former must be the aim of our undertaking. It is not temptation to evil destined to be overcome in order to earn some sort of fantastic bliss which steadies the will to do good, but . . . the resolve never to regret any of one's actions. That is what I would teach Antoine.

OCTAVE

And the method of this charming education?

ROBERTE

. . . Would consist in defying him to face up calmly to the consequences of his actions.

OCTAVE

So if ever the idea of murdering me or of raping you were to enter his head . . .

ROBERTE

If he were ever to feel that temptation it would be owing to nothing but your influence upon him, since here the boy is ready to believe that everything has been atoned for in ad-

vance by the Son of God. But, rid of any picture of a re-
deeming God, no such preposterous ideas could even occur
to him once he saw himself the prisoner of his own will;
there would be an end to any question of his exceeding his
limits; but his actions would take on such weight that there
would also be an end to any wavering between what is to be
done and what is not to be done.

OCTAVE

And in the event he is wrong?

ROBERTE

He will pay.

OCTAVE

May not you be the one who has to pay, Roberte? For by
virtue of what shall he be brought to answer for his error,
by what pact shall you have bound him which you'll be able
to accuse him of having broken? For him to learn never to
regret his actions he shall perforce have to fling himself into
the experience merely in order to find out whether he won't
regret them, not only because so long as you have not
drowned him in stupidity he must retain his susceptibility to
temptation, but also because the absence of regret will be
the very first thing to tempt him. On the other hand, if we
are forewarned that freedom drives our spirit to distraction,
is there any additional need for a demonstration of it? But
you, under the pretext of doing away with the presence of
evil and establishing good upon the absence of truth, you'll
have condemned human beings to suicide.

ROBERTE

You, Octave, you confuse the absence of a revealed truth
with the situation of the human being who has got to forge a

truth for himself because no God has revealed it to him, and which is then his sole veritable situation. . . .

OCTAVE

I defy you to demonstrate this distinction to us. . . .

ROBERTE

I accept the challenge, you have driven me to distraction.

OCTAVE
(*suddenly frightened*)

Roberte, you have nothing but a body to back up your word!

ROBERTE
(*letting out a curious laugh*)

And to keep it I have nothing but a spirit. (*And while Octave steals away from the room as if fleeing in apprehension of something too dreadful to endure, Roberte, apparently preparing to go out, begins to draw on one of her black gloves, addressing herself to Antoine:*) As for you, my little one, forget this conversation and, to borrow your uncle's terms, beware of falling into the clutches of pure spirits—a picturesque expression for designating the shadowy forces which honest labor and right reason dissipate and which will power defeats; beware of all the masks each of them may adopt in order to deceive us to the detriment of the unity of our personality. A soundly unified personality is not formed in the dread of an afterlife, but from contact with the community of mankind and in toiling in behalf of others: to satisfy the needs of those most handicapped by fate, the under-privileged, that is the most rewarding self-satisfaction we can seek, it is the only legitimate way of rising above our limits. Free yourself from the obsession of a dogmatic transcendence and discover a real transcendence in the brotherhood of practical effort: that is the only ethic which can possibly give meaning to this life. There is no pure spirit but the one which stands in solitude before a phantom of God; and then from the idleness of the will made for the sake of others, evil thoughts are born. . . .

She has still to come to the end of her sentence when Antoine sees Victor enter the room. And as the call comes from Antoine, "Don't talk, I want to see some more. . . ," Roberte turns about, stands rooted to the spot at the sight of Victor, and Antoine sees her thus in profile, one of her hands clutching a black glove, two fingers of her bare hand upon the other that is gloved which she keeps stiffly upraised in her amazement, her severe gaze fixed upon Victor who advances with a certain solemnity. When near, he seizes Roberte's raised and unmoving hand, removes its glove, and holding her fast by the wrist from behind raises Roberte's black skirt, bares her buttocks and begins caressing them. Roberte, dropping her other glove from her bare hand, tries to push Victor away and, seeing that he is making ready to speak, presses the palm of her gloveless hand over his lips. But while he fondles her buttocks, Roberte, shortly removing her palm from over Victor's mouth, gradually lowers her hand, straightens out her fingers, finds Victor's sedcontra, would thrust it aside and, without letting loose, leans slowly back.

VICTOR
(<i>holding her upright by the waist, and his hand
on Roberte's behind</i>)

Your gesture, Madame, proves that you believe a little less in your body, a little more in the existence of pure spirits.

And you will agree with us when we say that in the beginning was betrayal. While speech expresses things you judge ignoble from the mere fact that they are expressed, these things remain noble in silence: they have but to be accomplished; and if speech is noble only in so far as it expresses what is, it sacrifices the nobleness of being to things which only exist in silence; now, these things cease to exist once they begin to speak. How now punish the ignominy of speech? Has it not brought forth into broad daylight the flabbiness you vainly denounce as in itself obscene? Now as one knows little about false things except that it is true that they are false, because the false has no existence, seeking to know obscene things is never anything but the fact of knowing that these things are in silence. As for knowing the obscene in itself, it's to know nothing at all. For the lack of which, Madame, the words you censure have done nothing but fashion us a body which had been denied to us spirits; do you destroy the former, you affirm the latter in which the traitor is incarnated. Do you denounce him, you render homage to the glorious body in which your authors have clad us: "Eyes to dart the hot glance of lust, ears for the hearing of wicked speeches, a tongue to be the harlot of calumny, a mouth for the beckonings of greed, manhood to spend in unchastity, hands to dedicate to theft, feet to speed to crime."

Then, having twirled Roberte around only so fast as to give Antoine a view of his young aunt's buttocks, her thighs, the back of her knees and her long legs sheathed in black, Victor settles her upon his sedcontra, holding her by both wrists from the rear while she receives the major probation, perched on the tip of her toes. And as Antoine has fled into hiding behind a curtain, too moved to bear the sight, he is startled by a hoarse howl and made to look again: Roberte, her skirt still raised, with one hand seems to be adjusting her girdle or her stockings while with the other, holding them between the tips of her fingers, she tenders Victor a pair of keys which he touches without ever taking: for the two of them seem hanging in suspense in their respective positions.

THE REVOCATION
OF THE
EDICT OF NANTES

Take heed therefore how ye hear: for whosoever hath, to him shall be given; and whosoever hath not, from him shall be taken away even that which he seemeth to have.

—Luke 8:18

ROBERTE'S DIARY

February, 1954

Here I am, coming back to the dear old habit, contracted in childhood, of keeping a "free inquiry" notebook: those images of ten years ago are as strong as ever. Far from attenuating them, my married life with Octave only seems to be reviving them. He may take refuge in the confessional; but I, I know that I need no intermediary to make myself heard by you, O Master who were even loath to be called Good Master. What were those words of yours, that God alone is good? Were they to teach us to beware of goodness, of justice, and of truth, even if that means living . . . as idol-worshipers? Rather was it not to exhort us to dispense with any god in order to live good, just, and truthful lives? O Thou, disdainful of any idol, even to the point of liberating me from the one they have sought to make of Thee, would it be that Thou were putting us on our guard against an immutable goodness and justice and truth, the worst of all idolatries? And seeing as how none of the three can be separated from a god, does it not behoove us ever to search within ourselves for that which is good, just, and true? Thou whose death finally authorizes everyone to say: *I am the truth,* Thou whose crucifixion served to sanction the holocaust of new victims, Thou whose Cross guarantees the easy conscience of all the overfed and the extraordinary patience of the starving—here receive the fruit of Thy teachings. May I put your sublime saying into practice: *Let the dead bury the dead*—according to the interpretation I am here attempting to draw from it: Let dread for the past bury dread.

OCTAVE'S JOURNAL

*In gestu nonnulli putant idem
vitium inesse, quum aliud voce,
aliud nutu vel manu demonstra-
tur.*

—Quintilian, *Institutio Oratoria* (I.v.10)

January, 1954

"Some think there is solecism in gesture too, whenever by
a nod of the head or a movement of the hand one utters the
opposite of what the voice is saying." This passage from
Quintilian, quoted at the head of the descriptive catalogue to
my collection of paintings—to what does it allude? To what
I presume to be the motif of more than one of the unknown
master's pictures my collection includes.

At the outset one is rather hard put to make out the relationship established between gesture and speech; here are
certain gestures being made by the various figures represented, and that seems to be all. To what words do these
gestures relate? Probably to those the painter supposes said by
his personages, no less than to those the viewer may be saying
as he contemplates the scene. But if solecism there be, if it is
something *opposite* which the figures *utter* through this or
that gesture, they must say something in order that this
opposition be palpable; but painted, they are silent; does the

spectator speak in their behalf, in such a way as to sense the opposite of the gesture he sees them performing? There still remains the question of whether, having painted such gestures, the artist wished to avoid our solecism; or whether, from painting the kind of scenes he chose, he was, to the contrary, trying to demonstrate the positiveness of the solecism which could be expressed only through means of an image.

The type of woman our artist seems to have a particular affection for is that belonging to the latter half of the last century. Nothing surprising there: he was a little over thirty at the time of the Commune. "Affection" would here designate the feeling in the sole lover of his work, myself—though a man in his sixties—moved at seeing survive, thanks to his indiscreet brush, that race of Second Empire beauties whose prototype was incarnated by our Empress Eugénie (cf. Winterhalter) or represented by the early Monet's tall "Dame," or better still by the "Demoiselles de la Seine" of Courbet whom Tonnerre had joined in Geneva. Beauties of this species seem today to have been totally supplanted by the industrialized pin-up, the starlet sort, but here and there you see it crop up again, re-emerging from certain levels of society—O the fertile breeding grounds of High Protestant Society!—and it has already begun to exert its attraction upon the younger generation. One has simply to observe what is going on in my own house: Roberte, my young infidel of a wife, ruining our young nephew Antoine's peace of mind. . . . Unless I am much mistaken, they'll soon have had enough of their ideal, the "exotic" woman—to the devil with those beaches, those palm-tree "island paradises," hideous Gauguin, a curse on their *Fruits of the Earth!*—there will again be a sense for more sober, more reserved, in a word more classical physiognomies, for in us Westerners, the incurable heirs of Augustinian Manicheism, attractiveness resides in the austere appearance of the face, dissimulating— it's this that counts—all the more exuberant charms. (Canon V., my cousin, is perfectly right: he refuses communion to these bare-armed ladies, unless they are gloved to the elbow.) And our artist himself, as we shall see, seems to approve this emblem of dissimulation; the sly creature's trickery nicely agrees with the imposture of art, and with Tonnerre's art especially. In the motifs represented in the several pictures I have been able to salvage you recognize a propensity for scenes where the violence is due to a cunning unveiling—not to the unveiled, not to the nudity, but to the unveiling, to what is in itself the least pictorial instant. The eye likes to dwell restfully upon a storyless motif, and our artist seems to unsettle this repose of the gaze by suggesting to the mind what the painting hides. But as he is no less a thorough expert upon the space in which the object of his emotion is situated as volume, this suggestive vision comes from his skill at suspended gesture—one is almost prepared to believe he did his paintings after *tableaux vivants*. Indeed, though the *tableau vivant* genre is but one manner of rendering the spectacle life offers itself, what does this spectacle show us if not life reiterating itself in an attempt to right itself in the midst of its fall, as if holding its breath in a momentary apprehension of its origins; but reiteration of life by life would be hopeless without the simulacrum produced by the artist who, from reproducing this spectacle, manages to rescue himself from reiteration: such was, morally speaking, Flaubert's effort in his *Sentimental Education*.

To talk about the living picture in connection with painted pictures—it sounds like tautology. Isn't there always some preliminary *tableau vivant,* the basic antecedent to every picture? Yes and no. In the artist's mind the motif first passes through *tableau vivant* before getting on canvas. Here, in the case of Tonnerre, I am referring to the fascination exerted upon him by this in itself false genre, very much in fashion during the period. It was the reverse process that took place then; one generally drew one's inspiration from some well-known painting standing clear in everybody's mind, to reconstitute it, usually in a salon, with the help of those persons present, improvised actors, and the game consisted in rendering as faithfully as possible the gestures, the poses, the lighting, the effect one supposed produced by the masterpiece of such and such a painter. But this was not simply life imitating art—it was a pretext. The emotion sought after in this make-believe was that of life giving itself as a spectacle to life; of life hanging in suspense. . . .

ROBERTE'S DIARY (*continued*)

February, 1954

. . . How reconstruct the "grave offense" scene? In vain I reread what, once I had got over my emotion, I was able to jot down in the autumn of '44 at Rome itself. To be sure, I did misplace fragments just after the liberation of the city; back in Paris, I no longer had the strength to relate anything. These too burning images, I hoped to see them die out in forgetfulness; instead, they smoldered under their embers. . . . Some day or other I shall have to reassemble those "Roman Impressions," to take my courage in both hands and revive them one last time to be cured of them forever. . . .

(ROMAN IMPRESSIONS—FIRST FRAGMENT)

Rome, Autumn, 1944

I don't deny that to penetrate in such a way, my face disguised behind a mask, my hands gloved, but for the rest accoutered about as lightly as one could be, into this high-vaulted and dark place lit only by the weak glow of the night light, a first shiver ran down my spine—oh, an exceedingly agreeable one, something of a foretaste of what Vittorio was holding in store for me—naked in this spacious obscurity or rather ready to fling off the cape still enveloping me in order to bathe in the shadows upon encountering a hand. My presence here and at this hour, in this costume, was known, and I was by no means sure my gestures were not under observation; but if he who was charged to survey them was actually there, was he sharing my excitement at that very instant, and was he not also on the verge of losing control of himself? I was near to it, my heart pounding at the thought of the gesture I was to execute, already forgetting everything of this gesture's significance apart from the success or failure of my raid. In a word, the situation as well as my character was such that any presence or even the reality of an offense was farthest from my mind when I suddenly seemed to make out someone seated in the deserted rows and more and more to realize that the person there was a little old woman. She was not in front of me but behind, she could be watching me, and I was ashamed of myself. Steal away, or wait where I was? After a moment, she rose and went slowly toward the altar, where she lit a candle. As she struck the light I had shrunk back and ducked into a confessional, the only one that little chapel contained. No sooner was I inside —but who would have expected it at such an hour, long past the beginning of blackout?—than I heard a whisper through the grille: "Roberte, don't move." Reciting the formula I had been told to use in case of need, I ventured to ask, "Father, may I confess?" A sigh shortly degenerated into a muffled spasm of laughter: "You're just too lovely. Have you forgotten what there still remains for you to do?" "That is why I am here, Father." "What is the point of coming in that get-up to such a place as this?" I held my tongue, dismayed. From the looks of things I had stumbled on an informer; but he could just as well be on our side as theirs. "Take it easy," said the voice, "and don't forget your role." "My role?" ". . . is to produce yourself, with or without a witness. We've got to have these documents tonight." "What documents?" I asked, still pretending complete ignorance. "Relax, I tell you. We don't need to worry about the old lady." "Why should she worry us?" "Fear of the night patrols hasn't prevented her from fulfilling her vow. . . . Brace yourself, Roberte, to the fore and take advantage of the candle she just lit. She's already on her way out." "I am going, Father, give me your benediction." Then, getting up and starting forth, as I was halfway out of the confessional with one foot already on the stone paving of the sanctuary, my cape was snatched off. Thinking it had got snagged, I reached around and groped for it, but in vain; the questioning I had just been subjected to had thrown me off stride; the delicious sensation of those initial moments had given way to a numbing appre-

hension of having foolishly let myself get caught in something over my depth.

Immediately, the shadows seemed to teem with a thousand
staring eyes; at the foot of the altar the old woman's candle
shed an almost glaring light upon the tabernacle. Hugging
the wall, I stole up to the candelabrum and blew it out. And
the whole sanctuary was plunged back into its former obscurity to which the dim night light gave a tint of mauve,
when this misty obscurity suddenly appeared to condense into
a subdued glittering. By a pillar showed the contours of a
figure, a figure too huge not to be the semblance of another
world: leaning on the shaft of his halberd, wearing a Ren-
aissance lansquenet's outfit, his eyes flashing beneath the
visor of his helmet, completely unreal, as if having stepped
straight out of a painting by some old master to watch my
own unreality in this situation. Upon coming to the realization that this was a Pontifical Guardsman, all feeling of
seriousness simply drained out of me; caught up again by
that kind of ethereal light-headedness which had guided me
at the start—either the whole thing is doomed to flop or all
this is nothing but a dress rehearsal, I said to myself; isn't he
wearing a disguise too?—certain my mask would prevent me
from being identified, I held my ground and stared back at
him. Almost put on edge to see him stand immovable, his
legs planted wide, his doublet ending in a peculiar pouch at
his groin, I started to climb the steps leading to the altar;
keeping my eyes on him all the while, I fitted the key into the
lock of the tabernacle, opened its door; but off there in the
darkness he remained frozen in his position. I reached my
bare arm toward the tabernacle's silk-lined interior and with
my gloved hand touched the base of the sacred vessel: lifting
the chalice, I drew it out and groping with my other hand I

found the secret catch Von A. had mentioned. I pressed it
and a roll of paper emerged; I crooked a finger and slid it out
of its hiding place, folded it, and tucked it inside the opening
in the palm of my glove. Pausing there, again I waited and
once again scanned the shadows behind me. Then, losing all
patience with this stony indifference or with this handsome
fellow's insufferable standoffishness, I knocked over the
chalice, scattering Hosts right and left. At that same instant
the butt of the halberd came down once, twice, three times
on the floor; opposite me the tabernacle opened at the rear
and, dazzling white in the light streaming through from the
other side, two feminine hands, two slender hands whose
similarity to mine was frightening, advanced, seized my wrists
and held them in a grip positively of iron. Behind me the
huge person began to move, and his slow, almost processional
footsteps boomed in cadence with my beating pulse. Despite
my mask I didn't dare look back. "This is it," I said to myself, "this is what I was really looking for in coming here"—
for what was to happen from now on was to happen behind
me. I made an effort to get free and when I'd understood that
no amount of effort would help, my jitteriness turned into
something agreeable: I saw myself as I had been, walking up
to the altar, masked, gloved, half-naked, with the mad desire
to taste the consequences of my effrontery. And indeed, these
girlish, viselike hands holding me by I don't know what
power—the one I attributed to them—started to remove the
gloves from my own slender and flawless hands and having
turned them up, spread a salve upon my palms, moistened
my fingers to the very tips. But, trying to elude their burning
caresses, I fought away; already there, towering over me, he
pressed himself against my back and wedged me between his
breeches and the holy table. And, having brought the open

missal near, he applied my sticky palms upon a page of the Gospel; then, without letting go of me for an instant, he sprinkled some charcoal dust over the parchment and blew it away. My fingerprints were revealed and the lines of my hands stood out, printed there forever, upon the Word of God. . . .

"You who have insulted the Word, who are you?"

Aiming the beam of a flashlight at me, he saw me such as I was there: laced tight in my corset, shoulders, arms and legs bare. "A sad age we are living in," said he, "a sad age," and he tore off my mask. "Heavens!" he exclaimed, "behold it, the Paris to New York corruption!" And seizing me yet again by the wrists, he spun me around on my heels: "You're even better from behind than in front. . . ."

OCTAVE'S JOURNAL (*continued*)

March, 1954

Louvre this morning. Could not refrain from going for another look at Ingres, Chassériau, then Courbet, feeling it necessary to revive certain impressions in order to verify the context in which Tonnerre worked. The thing is to avoid being duped. . . .

Ingres's "Grande Odalisque" situates herself in a peaceful other world which provokes an aching resentment in the sorry souls we are. The "studio setting" surrounding her— we prefer to dismiss it as such—and which, "stagey" or not, suggests all the magnificence, painful for us, of the absent potentate, this setting is still the one thing able to provide us a rampart against an "unreality" which makes a mockery of our everyday worries and woes. "A moment in the studio, that's all it amounts to . . ." we protest in our poverty. The wealth of the departed sultan, it's just that which jealously envelops this marvelous creature; we see her on "vacation," supreme in her repose, pure of brow, offering us a few instants of the dorsal splendor of her unending torso, of her prodigious flanks, of buttocks and legs which leave us stunned; her glance searches us evenly while we guess at the volume of her breast from the shadow underneath her arm-pit, while we follow the elegance of the arm trailing along the heavy thigh presented "from below," while the idle hand, a fan between its fingers, lies, as though in waiting, upon the knee, the superposed legs, eye, lips, joints of the fingers as though put on the defensive by the strange rustle of our stare, coming from us who belong to the outside; from us others who, however, do nothing but reply to a murmur vibrating everywhere within her: a clamor sprung from her nape, which travels the length of her back, broadening out at the flanks to swell in the glory of her rump. But it is something we are not long able to bear and already seeking past the wonders of this body, our gaze strives to see it more alive. We think of the absent one, of the potentate, of him suddenly bursting in, we see the beauty's sovereign inaccessibility compromised in the gestures through which, from the sovereign she appears to be and from the height of her disdain for us, she will be brought low to the condition of a slave. We see her naturally resisting at first before gradually resuming her docile gestures, and this very resistance belongs of course to the series of "ritual" gestures. We see her, beyond the reach of us outsiders, submitted to the potentate's outraging caresses—all of them things which, however slightly one yields to antiartistic emotion, are to be seen displayed in this attitude of relaxation, the only one the artist shows us through a skillful structuring of the bust and the loosely held hip; all things from which we are barred by his art, accomplice to this splendor which keeps us at bay, which beats us far back from the explosive sight of what is about to befall the beauty, from that sight which Ingres's cold and unrelenting genius could not but scorn. That which he thus excluded from his visions hung around their edges none the less; it is the other way around in Delacroix's "Sardanapale," where this element, thanks to the pathos of that great painter, attains a somewhat too declamatory expression.

More moving for me is to see this element thrill in the nude figures of Chassériau, wrestling, one seems to sense, with compunctions as regards now the first, now the second of these masters. And I should imagine that Tonnerre, among whose representations I incline to prefer those which are devoid of "taste," must also have hesitated long before taking the plunge; alarmed at Chassériau's fate, but freed of the notion of the "sublime" by his association with Courbet, who showed him all the advantages to be drawn from the illustrative genre and from stereotypes of popular imagery, he deliberately rushed into the "bad form" so apt to afford me so much entertainment. Evidence of a hesitation between the sublime heroic and vulgar illustration would appear in his "Lucrèce."

Contemplating the scene, are we witnesses to the dilemma in which the Roman heroine is struggling? If she yields, she obviously sins; if she doesn't yield, she will be thought to have sinned, since, killed by her aggressor, she will be calumniated as well. Do we see her yield having first decided to destroy herself once she has published her defeat? Or has she first decided to yield, though it be to die afterward, once she has spoken? No question but that if she yields it is because she has been reflecting; had she not been, she would kill herself or have herself killed there and then. Now from reflecting upon her design for death, she throws herself into Tarquin's arms and—as St. Augustine insinuates—perhaps impelled by her own lust, later punishes herself for this confusion, for this solecism; which comes to succumbing to dread of dishonor, as Ovid puts it. She succumbs, is the way I would put it, to her own lust which splits in two: the lust of her own chastity separates from chastity and becomes carnal. But a truce to ratiocinations: for it all happens in a twinking of an eye, and it's the twinkle of a painter's eye. And our painter, what has he done? Only consider the adorable discretion with which Titian represented the scene: Tarquin threatens his prey with a dagger and seizes her by the arm. Lucretia, already bending, still implores. But what reserve in each of their attitudes! Let me be forgiven for mentioning Titian in connection with Tonnerre . . . anyhow, the latter shows us Lucretia lying full length upon a couch, propped upon one elbow, her head, seen in profile, erect, one leg straight, the other thigh lifting in a suspicious manner, as if repelling the aggressor perhaps, but preparing the way for him—the viewer will think; already lowered over her, Tarquin brings his face near the lady's cheeks, wrapping an arm around her waist, one hand clutching her breast the while she, her other elbow raised, her hand open, tries to fend off the young man's lips as the arm upon which she is leaning reaches down toward her belly where that hand, all its fingers extended, seems less to be covering her too visible shame than to be waiting. . . .

Such a composition would be incomprehensible to anyone unfamiliar with Lucretia's story, and that is what every painter should remind himself who still has the courage to treat a *subject*. To borrow assistance from the glamor the legend supplies beforehand, that is not enough; he must reinvest it with value by reinventing the scene—that is the line they'd take today. Nothing more trivial than a woman caught unawares and who puts up a fight while yielding or pretends to struggle while consenting. Typical of the abjection of those ignorant ones in our midst who pride themselves on their good taste: "Before all else, a painting is a grouping of blobs of color," etc. Lucretia? Ovid? St. Augustine? What are you talking about? Who's this Tarquin? Commit suicide?

Why, isn't that making a bit of a mountain out of a molehill? No, I'll not let them see this strange reptilian tangle that Tonnerre's canvas evokes; it is perhaps what he has brought off best in this composition, for having, precisely, been willing to be guided by the legend as it is set out in Ennius' version: *Mirabile dictu, duo fuerunt, et adulterium unus admisit*—it is this his brush has traced. But I return to the detail of Lucretia's panic-stricken face, to that hand which under the pretext of warding off Tarquin's greedy mouth, in the most flagrant manner presents her palm to it, to that other hand, lower down, which, far from forbidding access to the treasure, strains, reaches out its fingers. . . . What Tonnerre was endeavoring to express was moral repugnance and the irruption of pleasure simultaneously gripping the same soul, the same body, and he rendered this conflict through the position of the hands, one of which is lying and the other avowing a crime which seeps from its fingers.

The at once plastic and moral account to which Tonnerre turns the mimicry of hands struck me when, a great while ago, I first saw his "Lecture Interrompue." He must have devoted long study to the thousand and one ways in which the back and the hollow of the hand reveal either satisfaction or indifference as eloquently as surprise, irritation, alarm: just raise one or two fingers or bend them inward toward the hollowed palm or move the thumb away from them, and from what happens in the palm one reproduces an entire reflexive commentary upon what takes place elsewhere in the body, the inflection of the torso, the volume of the thighs, the lengthening and sweep of the legs, the position of a foot on the ground or hovering in the air.

The artist often enlarges his women's hands in order to emphasize what they feel; he thereby intrigues the spectator much more than when he exaggerates the legs and their curves. For, in placing the back of a hand in front of an unveiled fleece, in imparting this or that expression to fingers, in modeling the palm of a hand, in stressing index and thumb, he counterpoises a spiritual agitation against the tangible mass of this or that part of the body. And there, at that point, one can measure the exact degree to which the woman is in possession of herself or finds her charms slipping out from under the control of her will, we are witness to unending expropriations of the body subjected to an outside gaze and also to a budding complicity between the woman and an image of herself that she may have spent years combating: which explains the particular attraction of "the woman in her thirties. . . ."

ROBERTE'S DIARY (*continued*)

High time to have done with the Roman Impressions now that my public activity matters less to me than the very intimate task of schooling Antoine, our nephew. First it was my sister-in-law's death shortly after the war, then the emergency when my brother-in-law, a paymaster in the navy, succumbed to drugs in Indochina, leaving the boy a virtual orphan; since I have had no children with Octave, and cannot reasonably hope to get any from him, Antoine will be a brother and a son for me. The question is one of encouraging the greatest purity of intention in him, but also of having him see that inward stability is only acquired through acquitting our debt to the unlucky, of preventing him from making the mistake I committed along with my entire generation: the one consisting in confusing an adventurous impulse with a fallacious need for justice. But I am still putting off the moment of giving him a full welcome in the house. As long as anything remains of the Roman Impressions, Octave will have the edge on me in this competition that is as of now open between us and in which Antoine is the prize. My marriage to Octave may have been the last of my *faux pas*, imputable to the "grave offense"; and what I undertook and failed to accomplish at Rome—to save a guilty man in the midst of the uncertainties of war—I may have attempted again in Paris under other pretenses when I bestowed the prestige of my position—holder of the Resistance Medal, Commander of the Légion d'Honneur, member of the Commission de l'Intérieur—when I brought all that to this old man, spry despite his years, professor of an anachronistic science, canon law, and sacked from his university chair, this relic in whom there survive the bourgeois caprices of a bygone period which the disorder of our own has restored to fashion—I felt it was my *duty* to marry Octave. . . .

OCTAVE'S JOURNAL (*continued*)

Just what does contemplating such painted scenes satisfy in me? The pleasure available to all but which no one can take from looking at them in the presence of a witness? (For all breaks up at once into a thousand *all for one's self* . . .) It can be put in words of one syllable: these paintings, in the guise of art, realize precisely that which I am practically incapable of doing in life, with Roberte, although I don't shrink from practicing the thing without at all realizing it. Before a thousand glances these paintings reawaken the emotion aroused by a certain feminine physiognomy, they bring this physiognomy back to life, always in a new way, whereas my urge to pool the having of Roberte runs into a thousand obstacles: it isn't always possible to observe our rule of hospitality as well as one might wish. But, sometimes, it's enough for a simple anonymous glance to come to bear on Roberte, for that glance to make its lightning-quick inventory, its silent appraisal of her hidden charms for this taste of mine to be, not satisfied, but rendered sufficiently intense, pitched sufficiently close to perdition, irremediable in its intensity. Which is all that need be said touching the origin of the rule of hospitality that holds sway in our establishment. I told you so just the other day: the need for such rules isn't so readily to be understood, their mysterious sources aren't brought to light by a bald reference to voyeurism. A rare and precious object is not lent without the greatest reticences. But how is one to lend one's wife to other men? One cannot make up one's mind to do it without sensing a special thrill. You are disturbed by the term? That thrill too is shared among the husband, the wife, and the friends. Friendship itself is apt to stand in the way; a stranger, someone totally unknown, the least eligible kind of guest, would seem to lend himself a great deal better to the occasion. Excuse my employing this verb to lend in two different senses. But the following may clarify things for you.

Recently a young bank clerk came to see me on some business. Roberte, ordinarily out of the house at that hour of the day, lingered on in my study. Quietly listening to the explanations being given me, she begins to poke about through the papers on my desk; points a finger at a figure and brushes the gentleman's hand; goes on tapping her finger on the figure with the absurdest insistence. The young man, baffled, stares at her. I turn away for a moment to consult a folder of records in the cupboard. Raising my eyes I see that while he is pretending to be working over a column of figures she, perched on the edge of the desk, is leaning her chin on his shoulder and, as well, has slipped her finger beneath the young man's spread hand. Ascertaining all this, I close the cupboard and with an air of detachment suggest that he stay for lunch; we can discuss this sale and these purchases of stock over the meal. A few minutes later, the three of us at the table in the big dining room where, that day, I happened to have hung Tonnerre's "Belle Versaillaise" —Roberte, to my surprise, had decided to take lunch with us but in order to look as though she were pressed for time she'd kept on her hat, a charming hat—I ask this young fellow how he is getting on at his bank. It turns out that he has not yet been taken on the permanent staff there, that he isn't sure he'll stay, has a degree in political science and would like to do something along that line, that he has not tried for a Civil Service post but would prefer to find one as secretary to some member of Parliament. At that point I can foresee the turn the conversation is going to take and, noticing his glance stray to the painting on the wall, I ask him what he thinks of it. He wipes his lips and, swallowing a leaf of lettuce whose green contrasts with his freckled complexion, replies that "it's not bad." Would this individual who by all evidence isn't of my kind—he is now rolling bits of bread into spitballs between his long damp fingers—care to assist her with her voluminous correspondence? He could, Roberte proposes, give it a try for a week or so, for a start. He hesitates and very timidly thanks her. One can't however say he has accepted; Roberte's left-wing color and his own dependent connections with some personalities with more moderate views probably have something to do with this lack of enthusiasm. For my part, I conclude that the offer has been politely turned down, or almost. But, be it owing to my habit of inverting what people say or because the two of them have already reached an understanding in a language that isn't mine, lunch once over, Roberte steers him toward a nook adjoining the dining room where she has tentatively filed a part of her electoral correspondence according to zones and townships. He ventures a name, doubtless that of some moneylender. Why the instantaneous protest she snaps back with, as if this apparently harmless boy had made some insinuation? Leaning against the door jamb, she folds her arms. hooking one heel on the molding. He rattles on about this and that. But she, all the while keeping one hand tucked beneath her arm, advances the other, the fingers at first bent in toward the hollow of her hand, then unfolded and straightened, and touches the young man's tie. Disconcerted, he makes no attempt to interfere, then, when she moves her hand away, he catches at her wrist; and indeed she was holding a tiepin between her fingertips: "How ever can you let yourself be seen wearing such a frightful object!" she remarks, rotating the head of the pin between her fingers. In a daze, he squints at Roberte's gleaming nails which nip the pearl, he sees that pin lying upon the skin of her opened palm; it's now at both, palm and pin, he peers from closer by; and she shuts her hand upon the pin, sticks it back in his tie, adjusts the knot, smooths his collar. He shoots a nervous glance at me. But I, laying a hand on his shoulder, I ask him when he has to be back at the bank. His answer is that if I have anything else for him to give a once-over he could stay and tackle it now. I tell him he is the very person to inform me, and slowly draw the curtain. All that has to be done now is remove my eyes from the sight of that blue trouser-leg next to Roberte's silk-stockinged leg, of that masculine shoe nudging my wife's high-heeled shoe. And so my most dignified gesture is to retire into the hallway shadows. From here I gaze obliquely across the dining room to this curtain undulating on the threshold of the nook. Is this undulation to console me? Off in the direction of the foyer a ringing starts, a ringing too subdued to have been heard off in the servants' hall, it seems. All the same, it has a troubling sound in the hallway and I steal quietly back into the dining room when a new burst of ringing assails me, this time from behind and coming, no doubt about it, from inside the nook. The tip of Roberte's shoe skids out underneath the fringe of the curtain. And now her foot lifts off the floor, tangles in the fringe, the curtain comes loose from its wire. There indeed she is, sitting astride his knees and he is stolidly bouncing her, doing no more than bounce her although this is accompanied by a kind of voiceless incantation during which Roberte's blouse has fallen open. Odd, isn't it, that she, so reserved at the start and even distant in her offer of that secretarial job, so superior in that authoritative gesture of putting her hand to the anonymous fellow's tie, here she is tossing on his lap, tolerating the undesirable one's knee between her thighs, her legs dangling, her feet just grazing, no longer touching the floor, her shoulders already bare, freed of the straps of her brassiere which soon comes off altogether like the rind off a fruit, the two lace caps disclosing the rich and exuberant breasts. Seeing her hand still hunting for something to hold on to I think of all the time she devoted to her beauty care this morning, polishing and filing her nails while preparing her interpellation at the Assembly, whereas at the present moment with one of her sparkling hands, the palm pressed against this leech's face, she is still fending off but provoking his attempts to fasten on by giving him a foretaste of her satiny skin; meanwhile, leaning an elbow on the arm of the easy chair, she lets her right hand hang, idle. To think it required the ringing of this telephone, installed in the nook, for this delusively casual hand to spring into action, to grab the receiver, for Roberte to say into the mouthpiece that I was there. It was just then this wretched dullard, producing a sneaky heave of his flaccid body, had managed to bring Roberte's breasts down to the level of his buccal cavity while, seeing one of her nipples disappear into this lipless maw, she had herself reared up, one high heel skating on the floor, the calf of her right leg tensing, the other leg sweeping out to the side, kicking past the curtain, knee bending and raised high enough for this pig of a clerk, forgetting that he had been an utter stranger to this house two hours before, to take it into his head at last to give a little attention to the underside of that superb thigh, stroking it with the incredible complacency of a world-weary fop. Could it have been a melting sting of voluptuousness that made her open her hand and drop the telephone yapping to the carpet? Cover the short distance separating me from the nook, there would have been nothing to it—but profane this cheerless sanctuary? Intervene in this uninspired commotion, endeavor to give some brightening touches to this drab mess? Or instead, in the Russian style, hurl that fine vase like a wineglass against the mantelpiece? pull those folios crashing off their shelves? The smashing of china, the dry thunder of philosophy would have been wasted on them—for there was the telephone which rather than interrupting them —far from it—was spurring them into extra speed, making them cut corners, and at the same time was threatening to make a ruin of my dream. For a while I didn't mind letting the Canon's voice wind through the wire trailing on the floor and sputter out of the receiver into the empty air of our abomination. But the idea of answering the phone as if nothing were going on and in so doing call the undesirable one to order, it's this that brings me striding across the room, set on restoring things to rights. Had I overestimated the distance?—I brake to a halt, almost tripping over their entwined bodies. The receiver is lying under the easy chair upon which they are camped, the Canon's voice snuffling its indefatigable "Roberte, it's urgent!" What does this mean? Am I to go to the point of kneeling down before them? A cold courage steels me, I squat, stretch my arm under the sagging springs of the chair, grope for the receiver. Already flattening before the first gusts preluding the storm, Roberte has sunk low over the temporary employee's lap who is himself feigning a siesta, as though gorged on the treasures I alone am supposed to know. However, when I pronounce a "Hello" he jumps back to life, stands upright and, sending a half-swooning Roberte full length to the floor, he declares to me that I've caused him to waste his time . . . telling me this without bothering in the least to notice that I am putting a hand over my ear in order to hear the Canon's voice at the other end of the line confirm that I have been definitively excluded from the Faculty, that I had been given sufficient warning. And indeed: now standing up too, Roberte adjusts her hair, elbows uplifted, her armpits exuding her best natural odor; he, blowing his nose, cleaning and bending his glasses back into shape and—can you believe it?—insisting that I ring up the bank this minute and explain to his boss that I alone am to blame for his being late, that I couldn't decide whether or not to buy that stock, and that none of any of this is his fault! My reply is a blanket refusal and I invite him, on his way out, to step back into the dining room; there's where I count on getting even with him. Stopping him in front of "La Belle Versaillaise," I say, "You still haven't told me what you think of it"—and I'm all set to leap at the boor's throat. Having shrugged his shoulders and said, "She looks too much like your wife," the slap I give him sends his glasses flying. He staggers, stoops to pick them up; I get there first with my heel: "Blind despite his eyes, deaf despite his ears," I say as I dance around him. But he begins to shout, "Filthy old bastard with your whore for a wife!" and gives me a kick; I land half inside the cabinet housing our superb Venetian glassware. I'm completely covered with it, bits of wreckage are glittering even in my mustache. Alerted by the uproar, Justin rushes in from the servants' hall, lifts my aggressor like a pillow and is about to remove him to drop him out the back way when, sailing in like a fury from the depths of her bedchamber, Madame, very lightly clad, strikes the good Justin, wrests the vandal from his grasp and protecting him with all her untouchable charms, murmurs her apologies: ". . . I am so dreadfully sorry, so confused" while he whimpers on her naked shoulder—and, dragging him into the bedroom, she slams the door behind her. After which Justin rubs his cheek, takes his whiskbroom to my suit, clears my collar of shards of glass, relieved at not finding any cuts on my neck he rubs his cheek some more; mutters, "God, what a bitch!" and for the sake of form I draw myself up with a "Justin, about whom, may I ask, are you speaking?" to which he retorts: "About Madame, of course! About Madame!"—so many slips of the tongue requiring simply to be overlooked. And now, if you'll be so kind, tell me how to prevent other such collapses of a too hastily pursued vision? Is it that I am never clever enough at detecting the worthless ones among the accessories that turn up in the course of the day? But how else pass it if not upon this rushing stream of incidents to which in our weakness we entrust the frail little skiff of our nostalgia? Is it not legitimate to want to leave space for what we especially appreciate? But, that which we appreciate, where then are we to situate it if we are unable to create a living space for each and every one, we who are condemned to living amidst the meretricious appreciations of our fellow beings? Once again: the daily experience provided me by my collection of the unshowable works of an unknown master, isn't it a deceiving derivative of that very thing to which I aspire: the conversion into common property of an asset which for remaining incomprehensible is that much more immutable? I who have as a companion of my last years this creature concerning whose charms there is general agreement, must it then be she I sacrifice to the distraction of this unhappy world? Do I stand to gain anything whatsoever from seeing her treated like a security on the stock exchange? Shall I be punished for proposing her as a hint of riches to come? Must not this hint also fade away in order that these riches come? And still, you know, such making common property of a cherished living person is not without analogy to the hallowed gaze of an artist; to the prestige of the image he creates, death confers the authority of an eternal blessing. Life itself, the physical life of my wife may give the lie to the sincerity of my generous act: the wonderful bestowing of a gratuitously accorded pleasure, the vulgar call it the "favor" of a woman wilting from boredom; but no one discerns my emotion; it has no objective equivalent for this mercantile breed; it has no absolution to be in hope of; so it is valueless, unseemly, low. . . . The right way to be is to be jealous as others are.

ROBERTE'S DIARY (*continued*)

April 2, 1954

A woman anything less than furiously in love with her own body and who, wishing all the same to possess a man, seeks to conquer him by utilizing every spiritual resource doesn't really satisfy him: she even cheats him of what in her is by nature least exchangeable and quickly ends by incurring his warranted dislike; he isn't looking for an angel. How many are the women who commit such a mistake, obvious though it be! Your man has no use for thoroughly discouraging manifestations of fine feeling. Poor creature, don't you realize that in your very eagerness to show yourself generous, the more effusive you are, the more you exasperate your incomprehensible companion? We cannot compete with men on the grounds of masculine disinterest—unless we take on a saintliness in which we lose all our attractiveness. It's a strange confusion—the beautiful soul has no inkling of it—that arises in these women when coquetry remains alive enough to alternate with surges of self-denial, of voluntary and finally regretted self-deprivation. Afterward we inevitably resort to blackmail, but only claim due return when it is too late; in this regard, Octave has behaved with perfect honesty, although in him this is simply the better side of the coin that bears his perversity stamped on the other; I had to struggle for a long time against this taste for my own flesh which I'd lost starting in early childhood. . . .

A woman is totally inseparable from her body—the least scratch to our pride causes it to suffer—nothing is more essentially alien to us than the distinction drawn between physical and spiritual. We are in wholehearted agreement with men when they deny us a "soul" after having fraudulently appealed to our sentiments of honor and fidelity. But the insuperable misunderstanding begins with the idea that we are mere animals. Naturally hostile to being defined in terms of the spirit, woman views herself in terms of her corporeal sensibility alone, but—and this is the crux of the matter—her body is nothing else than her soul, and it doesn't make any difference either if she happens to be ugly: apart from the fact a physically ill-favored but intelligent woman wields an even greater attraction over men who immediately treat her as their equal, a woman who is ugly despite this dissimulation or this compensation is still woman enough to secrete the means a pretty girl disposes of; these means are always the same, and any man is capable of succumbing to them. And that is the answer to every one of the unfair oversimplifications concerning us in which men like to indulge; for them, we are never anything but to be had, to be slept with and to be despised because we only dominate them at the expense of the spirit. Yes, Octave, we are natural-born atheists; and atheism's progress in the world of today may perhaps have its true source here: the growing importance of the hand we are taking, the weight we are exerting in present affairs. Yet our basic refusal to *believe* is as different from that of a knowingly and determinedly atheistic male as the latter's bias is from the faith of a nun. I'll go still further: my own cousin, converted to Catholicism, today in a Ursuline convent, is nearer to me in her attitude than my friend Sarah, and out-and-out materialist. The feeling she has for her body, more profoundly inherent in woman than in man, is also the reason why she is better able to stifle the senses, to attain insensibility, than the ascetic; no more body, no more soul; perfect death; an extinction with which, however, we have an almost sweet relationship, a tender one; our nothingness is as *warm* as our body; *sang-froid* is nothing but virile vanity.

OCTAVE'S JOURNAL (*continued*)

Mid-April, 1954

How many times has not Roberte manifested herself to me in all the selflessness, the generosity, the saintliness that are naturally her own! How many times have I not had to fight against the image of her as soon as it emerged in that light! How many times, even as I immediately cast a pall over this radiance threatening to dissolve the meshes in which my foul daydreams hold her prisoner, have I not myself been driven to envisage the necessity for a complete overhaul in my behavior toward her! Could it be, I wonder, that another existence might have been possible for us, one in which the aim of my best efforts would have been never to cloud the limpidity of this soul until, secure behind the palisades of her unbelief, she'd of her own accord have come to recognize her self as the zone of grace? But as for awakening be it the bare suspicion of the dispenser of grace, how could I expect to have done it when my first impulse was always to hide its light under a bushel, as when having said my evening prayers on the sly in our bedroom, I'd no sooner have finished them and crossed myself, she'd have no sooner slipped into her shimmering full-length nightgown, than I'd be after her, prodding her with questions about some encounter or other that hadn't taken place? How many times I was on the verge of writing an end to this unconscionable disorder, abandoning this deceitful impunity! And then it would simply take, let's say, an outburst of perfectly childish laughter from her, and which from being sustained would be anything but childlike, it would take no more than a gesture of her too lovely hand for all this to fade out inside me, to my enormous and awful relief, and for the old light to bathe her whole physiognomy anew, in so doing modifying it; as if her soul, glimpsed an instant but upon subsiding into opaqueness again giving added emphasis to this body and further baring it to the risks its palpability implies, had become one with the skin sheathing this so widely solicited flesh, from then on present only in the quiver of shame, such a soul could not even have suspected to be dwelling in its recesses, this quiver by means of which it had come to reign over my senses, and by means of which I make it reign over others too. . . .

But of all this she can't possibly know anything, she'd not be able to delimit these different areas, for if she could she wouldn't really be what she is for me who destine her to others: the fact is that the purity wherewith she shines—and, no doubt about it, it is the fundamental ingredient in her nature which if left to follow its own course would lead her toward the simplest sort of life and the very opposite of the one I have given her—this purity is something she never detects or possesses otherwise than compromised, if indeed she ever happens to think about the matter at all. For the whole of her is engrossed in this continual oscillation between unequivocal purity in which the senses dominate and the impure throbbings I waken in her mind and whereby the very name of her assumes this fascinating coloring she has in my eyes. But, for her part, it's in defeat alone she perceives her dignity, shattered in defeat. And, too, this image of self, mirrored in the stare others turn upon her, only comes to her when inside her there wells up the irresistible urge to break loose and live, which she thinks she is obliged to curb, an urge to be free of her dignity, of this dignity that seems engraved in the regularity of her features. But let her just start to set it aside and, more beautiful than ever, let her austere countenance turn into the hollow mask of that dignity, and she, giving rein to her senses, acquires my attitude of mind; whereas the crudely flattering stare of others, when it roves over her, assessing her body, her hands, her legs, strips her of everything down to this mask which she'd like to go on maintaining, and only restores it to her along with the opinion pronounced upon her; this mask she cannot henceforth continue to maintain without enlisting the aid, unworthy of her, of this stare which a moment ago was foreign, which is hers as of now.

That is where my reprehensible intervention occurred as I progressively developed in her both this sense of self and the kind of conduct toward which I inclined her; for she had to be trained into an awareness of this to and fro, of this way of letting her at first overly attentive body go through a reflex to which she was not accustomed, and for a long while I did nothing more than impute this consciousness to her, lending her mine and being careful to take my time before demanding that it precede the very least of her gestures.

Surely, every movement of her head, flutter of her eyelashes, pursing of her lips, play of her fingers was bound up inseparably with this sense of her self. But from there to getting her to picture herself in advance, to have a preview of herself, when she was seen and a stranger was eying her? To inciting her to detach her gestures from this sense of self without ever losing sight of herself? To having her attribute them to her reflection in another's gaze, to the point, as it were, of mimicking herself under another's dictation but without ever once thinking she was acting in obedience to an outside will? To fostering the illusion she was acting on her own initiative in order that she afterward feel more fully ashamed at having caught herself in her own trap? To giving her, finally, a liking for the flavor of this shame so that she subsequently contract the habit of satisfying her taste for it? To be sure, the deep-seated need to give herself, common to every woman, offered a ready-made springboard for launching my experiment. But what made its success altogether hopeless was that this same need, being too natural, was apt to remain in the vicious circle of nature within which not only the habit of domestic life, but ordinary good manners, with all their inhibiting accompaniments, always have the effect of imprisoning the senses and thereby prevent their access to the mind. That Roberte acquire a fondness for herself, that was the thing, that she seek to discover herself in her whom I was elaborating from her own elements, and that gradually, through a sort of rivalry with her own alter ego, she even come to want to improve upon the aspects which took first-draft form in my mind; it was therefore important that she be constantly surrounded by young men looking for amusement, by idle males. Now for quite some time I had the feeling that in all the various circumstances under which this game was played or seemed to have been played through to the end she was not fulfilling all its rules; instead, I tend to believe she never gave herself without the firm conviction that she was doing her duty, never at any rate without thinking that she was handing me proof of her attachment. But who then was being wronged? So long as she acted out of devotion alone, wasn't the experiment a failure? If on the contrary the experiment was already over with and she was moving ahead on her own, where might we be heading? Was Roberte on her way to breaking loose from the chains I'd forged for her? The outcome was completely different. She went right on acting out of duty, but in her eagerness to satisfy its demands finding she disposed of resources which she would have considered abhorrent before.

The fact we had not had children couldn't help but have its impact upon Roberte's inward structure although she might have been willing to forego the satisfaction of her desires for motherhood. These aspirations are usually held to be insurmountable. I don't belong to that school of thought. One may allow the possibility not only of a transmutation but of a real and superior compensation by something else which commonly seems to disappear when maternity sets in. Unless every feminine nature is at all times maternal, which, for me, just amounts to a figure of speech. This something else I have in mind here is a sororal aspiration, doubtless of a virile cast within the feminine framework; and which, while not maternal in the empirical sense of the word, is on that very score all the more eminently a tutelary quality, along with being a capacity for association to evil ends as well as to good; and it doesn't much matter which. In Roberte this tutelary quality was intimately related to her need to dominate; this capacity for association, on the other hand, had to do with something less transparent. In it could be made out the need to take on form which spurs every woman to seek a yoke of some sort or other. The aim of the sororal propensity, when all is said and done, is to exert power over another person, this on a plea of protecting him. But through what is this power exerted if not through the image the woman has acquired of herself, an image she can never obtain except after having surrendered herself, with everything malleable in her, to an as yet unknown master. The extent to which these two tendencies may conflict, the extent to which they may become entangled, the one forever striving to take rise from the other, one has a good picture of it in Roberte evolving in the curious constellation of our domestic life.

ROBERTE'S DIARY (*continued*)

May, 1954

. . . I leave Octave to his ratiocinations and his prayers: that he have the inconceivable arrogance to imagine himself responsible for my misbehavior, why, I don't mind at all—but as for supposing that he is at the origin of my temperament . . . The poor old dear hasn't the faintest notion of what I am capable of without any help from him; even though he wear himself to a frazzle conjecturing what happens to me and inventing what he'd like to see me experience, I'll never tell him about the things that have actually happened to me and may well happen to me some more: one word to Octave and Antoine would find out the next minute. The boy wouldn't get another night's sleep.

Formerly I'd never have dreamed of reverting to such things. Those due to Octave, I mean. But at present I cannot refrain from retelling myself the story of this or that episode (which occurred unbeknown to him): nothing more vulgar, but since *it* happens to me and keeps coming back to me, by writing it down I may be able to get it out of my system and not have to think about it all day long. *It* was preying on me this morning at the Committee session, I couldn't collect my thoughts; nobody noticed, but just the same . . . even taking a bath, as I did the last time, isn't enough anymore. A violent feeling of shame—can a woman still go seeking for it once she is a respectable member of society? It's an image: brooding over it has been keeping Octave's mind busy for quite some time. This quest is surely an unreality, that's my view; or would it be my respectability that drives me to it? I remember I felt ashamed; did I enjoy it any the less? And now, in the memory I have of it, my own shame is not so distasteful to me, the less so since I see myself as such as I was able to please those individuals. . . . Is that to say they'd have some importance owing to this fact? The next time a similar situation were to recur, if I am still honest with myself I must confess I won't resist; and this brings me (as just a short while ago) to finding as much enjoyment in my dishonor as in those who dishonored me. . . .

. . . After I came out of the manicurist's in the rue Scribe, Justin, who was waiting for me, couldn't get the Buick started. This didn't really inconvenience me, I had time to kill before returning to the Palais Bourbon and, having scheduled no appointment that would interfere, I decided to take advantage of this mild and wonderfully sunny afternoon. I hopped on the rear platform of a bus, the first that came along, and was leaning against the railing, dreamily watching the shops go by, when some peculiar touching obliged me to go and take a seat inside the bus. . . . As he persisted in staring at me, I stood up and got off at Théâtre Français. Walking through the Palais Royal gateway I entered the Galérie de Montpensier. Beneath the arcades, practically deserted at that hour, footsteps echoed mine, drew nearer; as can happen any day to a Member of Parliament, I was being followed. The fellow in question, a very big man, tall, beefy, smooth-faced, a good sample of the sort that does a little spying on the side for the police,

keeps two or three steps away from me and stops each time
I pause to glance into a display window. Where on earth is
this new lingerie shop Gilberte told me I ought to visit?
I turn and start down under the Galérie de Beaujolais: there
it is, on the right. But now the fellow overtakes and passes
me. I push a plate-glass door, find I'm in the wrong shop
—this one is just in the process of being converted—the
fellow enters too. Even though the people who are strolling
outside or standing in front of the bookstore across the way
have only to look hard through the partially smudged win⌐
dows to detect anything abnormal that might be transpiring
in this empty shop, nobody thinks to for one instant. His
back to the glass door, the giant blocks my path when I
attempt to leave, reaching my hand to the doorknob. Then,
through a door in the back of the shop, appears another man,
of less than medium height, thickset, in his shirtsleeves.
They give each other the eye. The second retreats behind the
counter and leaves the inner door ajar. . . .

. . . Less than an hour later I sit down at a table on the
terrace of the Régence, the blood throbbing in my veins.
My hands are probably shaking and the waiter asks me at
once if everything is all right. I smile, get up to go to the
washroom, peer at myself in the mirror: no point taking
out my compact, I look fine. When you come right down
to it, what exactly is there to blame them for? If it gave
them some deplorable pleasure . . . For me, it's now that
the pleasure begins. I return to the terrace and I go through
it all again. When on the platform of the bus I'd been leaning back against the railing, my forearm and hand resting
on the edge of it, the giant, who had been talking to the
conductor at first, had taken hold of my fingers. I'd gone
inside and chosen an unoccupied seat; but he, who had come

in and sat down opposite me, had started that rude scrutiniz-
ing. I was sitting with my hands spread flat on the leather
seat-covering, my legs separated perhaps, and a smile was
straying over my lips while the warm breeze blew in at me
through the lowered window. Had I kept that smile, my
lips parted, while his stare was becoming more insistent?
I at least crossed my knees immediately and folded my hands
on my lap. After all, I had my Légion d'Honneur rosette
in the buttonhole of my jacket. That was the moment when
I decided to get off the bus and, I remember, I pulled the
rosette loose and dropped it inside my handbag. I non-
chalantly crossed the Place du Théâtre Français, I entered
the Palais Royal, and so on until I was under the Galérie de
Beaujolais vaulting. . . . And then I try to retrace the
fellow's itinerary, stage by stage. He liked me. It was too
much for him, he had to touch my fingers and from then
on there was no stopping all the way down to the cellar.
Beginning with that furtive but irrepressible touch he gave
me, what must have been the scenario, rapid but also mi-
nutely detailed, that unfolded in his brain? Or else had there
only been a vision of those parallel bars the whole length
of the route, and the fear lest the day end with them remaining unused and put in readiness for nothing? When
afterward he found himself sunk to the floor in front of me,
reduced to impotence, the two images, that of the fair
stranger wearing the rosette in her lapel and that of the
same woman, suspended at last and tied, did the one substi-
tute itself for the other to the point of coinciding, or was
the contrast between them such as to have been the cause
of that excitement which swelled his sad face? Once off the
bus, after having trailed me from a short enough distance
to be able to see me strolling ahead of him under the Palais

arcades, having already "contacted" the epidermis of my fingers, he must have elaborated this initial sensation, extended
it to the whole of my body he was concentrating upon, stud-
ied the sway of my hips, my eventual poses in the imminent
situation which he knew would be entirely new to me, inconceivable and therefore, for him, all the more imperative . . .
until the moment when he had no choice but to nab me
inside that empty shop. How he looked, almost dazed, at my
hand on the knob of the door he was preventing me from
opening while the thickset one was materializing through the
door in the back, that fatal door left ajar and on the other
side of which the secluded staircase wound underground.
Noticing an exit on the landing above and which probably
gives out on to the rue Beaujolais, I turn to make a dash for
it. But the shorter man, who was waiting for me on the steps,
aims a blow of his hand at my fingers clutching the railing;
and I, still thinking escape is possible, I pull them quickly
away, redescend and—almost in reach of the door leading
back into the shop, just as I, still determined to put up a
fight, hit the giant in the face with my handbag, I see him
go down, really, he nearly crumpled . . . when that same
instant his hand slips between my garters and my flesh, takes
a firm hold on my thigh, his arm wraps around my legs, he
lifts me, tilts me forward over his shoulder, this happening
so unexpectedly and so swiftly that I had to hang on to his
neck with both hands—and then that fantastic trip down
the spiral staircase to the basement. The other one, who had
preceded him, was by now opening the heavy steel door
beyond which lay the big room, lit by neon and with dazzling
white walls. The floor was gleaming linoleum; enormous
ventilation fans started turning overhead; and in the middle
of an assortment of physical training apparatuses there were

some parallel bars, straps attached to them. . . . Just to think that a short while ago I was sauntering idly between the Opéra and the Théâtre Français while these bars were awaiting me here all the time! So then, fastened by the wrists, my moist hands diffusing the scent of their lotion in the air, stifling despite the ventilators, my fingernails faultless and useless . . . Without concerning themselves in the least about my bust or bothering to take off the jacket of my gray suit, they unhook my skirt and remove it along with the rest underneath. I'm still prancing my feet; they bind each of my ankles to the uprights—and all this in silence, a silence composed of my own muteness almost attuned to the two men's, as if our pantings were replacing whatever words we might have exchanged here. The giant's mouth approaches one of my bound hands and I having doubled it up into a fist, he pries open my fingers, passes their ends between his lips and lingeringly tastes each of my fingernails. Then, after a pause to catch his breath, reeling on his feet, sweating, holding on to the bar, he sticks out his tongue whose tip curls up in a miserable effort and only manages to slowly brush my wide-open palm. Finally though his tongue stiffens and begins its ever more rapid titillations. I still have my head turned aside. . . . Soon it is too much for me to contain myself any longer, in vain I try to raise a knee, to hide the irresistible effects with my thigh. "Then get rid of those lights!" I say in a voice that isn't mine anymore while the smaller one, planted opposite me, ostentatiously displays a visiting card and slips it into my bag. But the lights stay on and, my eyes shut, under the whirring of the fans, I abandon myself in front of these two strangers. . . . The assuagement I then feel from opening myself at last, from unpenting myself before their stares in this impos-

sible position . . . A dull thud at my feet. I open my eyes.
The giant has collapsed. The short fellow hoists him up
by the shoulders and holding his sagging frame erect, leads
him away. For more than a minute I remain there, bound,
alone—doubtless the least pleasant moment in what I can't
even call a nightmare. And it's almost with relief I see the
second one reappear, slowly, hands in his pockets—a blond
lad, with a crew cut, with prominent eyes, an intelligent
gaze. His shirt was neat, spotless, and his hands, which he
now took out of his pockets to detach me, carefully groomed;
he had a silver bracelet on his left wrist. He looks the other
way while I readjust my skirt, goes to fetch my handbag and
bringing it to me also offers me a glass of cognac. But I
slap him. Whereupon, with a single gesture, he snatches
off my skirt again, stands a foot on it, puts his hands back
in his pockets and, without flinching, receives another slap;
and here I am, and I lose consciousness before I am able to
stop. . . . What could a woman be expected to do in such
a situation . . . ? Scream, obviously, bring the whole building running—in such a busy section of the city—but we,
the women who rode in the Red Cross vans, on "the
front lines of charity," we, the women who are now at the
helm of the nation, we women who "have been around"
and through too much—if ever we be fair, if ever we have
retained our beauty—we can do but one thing, and that is
say nothing. Make an investigation? Because of this card
which reproduces . . . my fingerprints? Get to the "bottom" of it all? Just the sort of job that bungling C. at the
rue des Saussaies is cut out to handle? Nonsense. But, one
of these days, to revisit the scene, to stroke those parallel
bars with my hands, those bars where my hands were so
firmly bound . . . that's another story. This special occa-

sion for feeling my own self from the instant I jumped aboard that bus until the one, in the basement, when I woke up to find myself spread-eagled and shaken, this occasion is now neither more nor less than the bow which sends my thoughts soaring high above this lazy afternoon. What delicious croissants they serve here! How soothing, those fountains splashing under the sycamores! How exquisite this city is as it glides gently downhill!

OCTAVE'S JOURNAL (*continued*)

May, 1954

The hours I waste while she is away, imagining her poses, the very least of her poses, it's simply inconceivable. And to think that in the meantime she herself is hard at work, making decisions, carrying on an activity which not only answers the requirements laid down by the life of present-day society, but can as well merge into and re-emerge among all the underhand pettiness spawned in parliamentary locker rooms —and all that without a care in the world for my own moss-gathering inertia! Suppose I had pursued my career to the pinnacle of distinction and honors, and shown, I also, sufficient energy and a little more zest for satisfying the wearying obligations of an official existence, what would she have done? The same thing she is doing now: with our more or less similar ideas, we'd have been as solid a political couple as any going. What insipidness, good lord! Better that things be as they are now: Madame takes care of everything all by herself, sits in Parliament, in the Ministry of Information, participates in soirées and in short spends enough time out of the house to furnish me, staying put in my study with all the security needed under this unheard-of Fourth Republic, matter for interpreting as I like the reasons for her wee-hours-of-the-morning returns. Madame wages the good fight for brotherhood, for world-wide democracy; I just live and die for the sake of beauty and hence for the cause of the mean sons of bitches in this world.

O blessed age when Daguerre with his cumbersome and daring instrument fixed the image of that life, caught the daily life of that period then about to be stricken by the disfiguring austerity of the early industries, but which had not yet lost anything of its somnambulistic gait and bearing. What fascinates us at the sight of these pictures hovering between black and white is that they seem to open secret windows upon the working day of those times: at the moment a certain façade casts a certain shadow on the road, perhaps Balzac or Baudelaire or Delacroix has just stepped in or out of the doorway. The pace of business didn't exceed the trot of horses, an animal cadence, nor the respiration of human beings. Even in its trickling away through the hour-glass, time's passing was no more inexorable than the slow growth of shadow creeping over objects. People and things were yet able to assume a contemplative attitude before the gaze of this photographer who with the help of the attenu-ated accidents of light strove in quest of timeless structures. But thanks to that fatal conspiracy between cunning banker and cunning inventor, an unleashed energy, raising thought's aggressive tenor tenfold, a hundredfold, interfering with the factors of time and space, causing weight to evaporate, dis-locating structures, converting solid into fluid, rendered du-bious the presence of figures and objects in more and more fugitive space. Even the naive perceiving of them was dis-turbed: the Impressionists in this period echoed the swan song of the old day and the old night already modern: a supreme resplendence . . . and then everything disinte-grated in luminous dust—while in Provence an old demon, in love with the barren mountains and the rustling pines and eucalyptus, toiled to reconstruct the solemn aspect of the world once again. He was called a madman, but they who endeavored to follow the guidance of his divine hand wanted to remake their eyes into his without having his soul. In an atmosphere convulsed by strange trepidations, furious vibrations, centrifugal forces burst the eye and what it looked at: the yearning now was after explosion itself, and henceforth the gaze could only be satisfied by broken objects, by images gone to pieces; at which point the devil stepped in and, borrowing the voice of a heretical doctor if ever there was one, he proclaimed: "Photography has freed painting from the need to imitate nature."

ROBERTE'S DIARY (*continued*)

October, 1954

. . . Instead of letting Antoine languish in an institution where he was pining away under the regime, the alternative was to have him join us here, and did this not imply a challenge at a time when Octave had a witches' sabbath going full tilt in the house? I have the right to hope that the lad's presence will cleanse the atmosphere, hold Octave in check. There has already been a marked change. In Antoine, Octave finds a malleable as well as receptive pupil: the old professor's pedagogical appetites have been unsatisfied since being deprived of his university following, he now sees the means at hand to form a disciple. However, the Assembly is in session and my duties are claiming an ever greater share of my time; I'm hardly the homemaker anymore. This is not failing to make a grave impression upon Antoine. If I am gaining authority in his eyes, Octave, little by little . . .

OCTAVE'S JOURNAL (*continued*)

Let's have a look at Tonnerre's "Lecture Interrompue." Sitting in a chair, a young woman wearing a dark dress, her bust encased in a tight-fitting tucker buttoned up to the chin, one arm bent, with elbow resting on the arm of the chair, and holding a little book open between her fingers; the other arm, swung across and in front of her, starting up in a defensive gesture, the hand halfway opened: her legs crossed, the upper one slightly lifted, the hem of her skirt bunched up past the knee to the start of the thigh from where, rumpled at this point, her dress falls in heavy folds. Crouching against the young woman, to the right of her (to her left in the painting) a child of eight or ten, with a large head, a fringe of hair lying in bangs upon its forehead, with the eyes and grin of a perfect imbecile, dressed in a little jacket, has slithered one hand into the young lady's underclothing; a gesture her raised knee was to have parried, the position of the leg suggesting the involuntary reflex, while with his other hand the child has managed to unbutton the lower part of the blouse as high as the breast that has promptly leaped into view, blossoming through the opening, the frothy disorder of the slip contrasting with the chaste contour of the other breast properly in place inside the blouse on the other side.

Plainly, from the way in which the painter has treated and situated him, the child is of secondary importance, an acces-

sory. His subversive curiosity interests us only insofar as it
motivates the young woman's agitation: accountable for his
good behavior, she, rather than intimidating him, by her
captious presence provokes what it was her job to prevent.
Her ward's gesture brings her to grips with herself and makes
her recoil into herself: so that *seen* otherwise than she ought
to be seen, she is showing herself despite herself; an animal
but adult intention springs toward her in the shape of this
shameless little hand reaching for her breast, a breast whose
full curves are hardly made for these schoolboy fingers.
Perhaps she had been reading some too childish fairy tale or
a lesson for the boy to recite all the while his imagination
was at work, spying at her from behind a simulated attention. All this is expressed in the governess' sparkling eyes, by
this quiver beginning to pucker her lips. But what is more,
this movement of her arm changes her back into a woman,
suddenly become the object of an appetite of whose monstrous presence she had been totally unsuspecting. It's that
her hand declares, hovering on a level with her chin, it's that
the hollow of her hand declares, with this voluptuous root
of the thumb, these long fingers which seem skilled at much
more than punishing, than guiding a difficult child; a hand
trembling in recollection of some possible adventure while
the other hand, only the back of which is in view, its fingers
holding the book, still belongs to a state of responsibility,
so adorably denied by the hand grown wide and long in the
panic created by the little mischief-maker. Her lifted knee
reveals a well-turned leg, disclosed to the garters lying upon
her flesh whose warm tints contrast with the metallic sheen
of her silk stockings.

This picture is not among the painter's best as regards
composition. Proof thereof is that too many words come to

mind as we look at something that should reduce us to silence.

Once again, the movement of the face-high defensive gesture contradicted by that of the lifted knee. Sitting quietly reading a moment ago, now she looks as if hurled into her chair where, as if cornered, her reawakening senses bring knavery into her eyes. But in the prospect offered to the small boy, a prospect the painter re-establishes for the benefit of the spectator, the lifted knee thrusts the stockinged leg into the foreground; in the bend behind the knees appears the mass of the thighs where they meet the buttocks, an excuse for painting the luminous flesh between this secretive fold of the undergarment and the dark reflection of the silk on the calf.

ROBERTE'S DIARY (*continued*)

And so who has Octave selected for Antoine's tutor? Vittorio! How, where was he even able to meet him? At Dior's, where I'd narrowly avoided him. Salomon, the photographer, had introduced him to Octave as the fashion correspondent for certain Italian magazines. In the course of the conversation Vittorio mentioned the name of Z . . ., the Lausanne art collector through whom Octave obtained the paintings of Frédéric Tonnerre. They were launched; Vittorio said something about his "Vatican background" and right off the bat my fine Octave decides that this boy, so wonderfully combining the principal contemporary insanities, was as if sent by the hand of God to initiate Antoine into them! That is, Octave hasn't the barest inkling of what links me to this ghost from the past: the "grave offense"! Just as Vittorio was of course unaware that I'd become the most prominent woman in the radical party and, over and above that, Octave's wife. Then the inevitable introduction, one well imagines what it was like: Vittorio, remarkably elegant, just as remarkably self-controlled, did not so much as blink—while I had to hang on to the back of a chair. My chilliness may have betrayed me, and Octave immediately drew the conclusion that hostility was its cause; so much the better. According to his custom, he left us alone together. Whereupon Vittorio fell at my feet: "Do with me whatever you wish." I told him that our acquaintance dated from the moment

he had entered my house; that I considered his present identity irrevocable, though M. de Santa-Sede might no longer
exist. If he abided by those instructions he need expect
nothing from me beyond indifference and forgiveness for
the rest. That it was certainly sheer folly to entrust Antoine
to him—but that I counted upon his common sense, which
could only dictate strict silence to him. That I wasn't even
concerned to find out how he had escaped from the Germans
in Rome and then from the Allies. In this he made out a
threat and retorted in a dully aggressive tone that neither was
he curious to know what fate I'd reserved for Von A. and for
his victims. That was the instant when he flipped open his
cigarette case. Reaching for a cigarette, I had time to make
out the facsimile of my fingerprints engraved inside the
cover. I stopped speaking and he was able to feast his eyes on
my pallor, but his caddishness had given me the strength to
take a quick grip on myself: I replied that he had simply to
choose between no telling what revenge that would turn out
to be double-edged, and the conduct his position as Antoine's
tutor prescribed to him. He insinuated that never, of course,
would he have had the audacity to accept Octave's offer had
there been any possible way of knowing that he was to find
me in this house; that, most fortunately, he had snapped at
it in complete innocence and that as things had turned out
he was enchanted with his new post; that he marveled at his
good fortune. But that, knowing me in the way fate had
decreed, he absolutely could not forego trying his luck. He
grew bolder and went so far as to express the hope that the
sensations I had procured him and that I had experienced in
return ten years ago in Rome under the trying circumstances
of war might sooner or later be renewed here in this very
peaceful, very agreeable setting of my home. I rose to tell him

to get out of the house that instant: and indeed his charm was still able to outdo his insolence. "You've come a long way," said I, turning my back on him; "keep going," I added, pointing to the door. But he had already folded me in his arms: "I have nothing more to lose," he said, "unless it's you." And he lay his hand on my hip, from where it went resolutely to my behind. "This," he cried, "belongs to me!" At the same moment Antoine entered to present himself to Vittorio. By then I was at the end of my tether. "Antoine," I said, the while not quite knowing what I was doing, "here is Monsieur de Santa-Sede who is going to devote his attention tò . . . you, so that you'll get by those college entrance examinations." "Those college entrance examinations!" Vittorio chimed in. "How long must we wait for the school reform act? Madame, when will you vote it through?" "Not before Antoine has passed his general studies." "But it is downright cruelty, isn't it, Master Antoine?" No sooner had my nephew withdrawn than: "Why have you told him I'm to be his tutor? I was ready to leave for good and never darken your door again . . ." And so saying he caught me by the waist. But then, pulling him into a remote bedroom where it suddenly occurred to me to lodge him: "I see through your little game," said I. "Since you're here now, you're going to stay. My room is at the other end of the apartment, but I'm never there until about two in the morning." "At your orders, Signora." I touched a finger to his lips. "Watch your step, my friend. You don't budge from here without my knowing about it. You will come to me only when I call you."

OCTAVE'S JOURNAL (*continued*)

No question but that it's the aspect women have in public, their way of making themselves seen to the outside and not as they are when at home, which constitutes that certain something whereby they derive their power to intrigue me. It is also during those moments when they want somehow to make an appearance abroad and neutralize their contact with the exterior, with the unknown, the alien, the anonymous in which however they sometimes seek themselves—finding what they were by no means looking for—that I visualize what is most charming about them, that I have the clearest glimpse of their start of surprise, their gestures in those unforeseen predicaments which tend to engross their so-called woman's day. And how these predicaments abound at every turn, how, each time, everything conspires to imperil their integrity, to jam the machinery of their resistance! By which I mean the integrity, the resistance they put into maintaining the routine of their woman's day! Oh, the countless little circumstances an idle individual need but put his mind to it to be able to exploit! Ah, if everybody in this world were like me. . . . There you have the explanation for this incredible restlessness which grips my ancient bones whenever Roberte goes out in Paris. To go out in Paris! In those five words space and time fall out of joint. . . . And chance, if it's not something else, would regularly have it that Roberte elect the most hazardous itineraries in the city. To be sure people nowadays have too much on their hands to attend to, too many cares weighing on their minds, are in too much of a frantic rush to wait around for a half-forgotten daydream to suddenly materialize. And yet it is equally true that Parisian life—and here is its primary attraction for the foreign visitor —has in every branch of activity, and in the most commercial, contrived to preserve room for the image of pleasure if not for its concrete practice. It's this which, as a direct result, gives pleasure its commercial character and which, through the very vulgarizing of pleasure, tends to rule out the situations I am thinking of, reducing almost to zero the number of individuals capable at the present time of making something out of them; far more than ever before, on the sidelines of the bleak battlefield where the struggle to earn a living is waged, immense hoards of boredom accumulate here and there, with these loitering individuals to guard them. What now is surprising about the fact that it be our elementary and high-school children who serve as their go-betweens since every sixth grader knows how to find the cash to go and play the pinball machines at the corner tobacco shop—was Roberte's observation, this being a point where for once I was able to agree with her, not yet having any idea that she herself was enough in agreement with *it* to have taken a fling at it, in, moreover, a strange and religious manner for someone of such laical dispositions. What cause has one for surprise indeed, I'd add, seeing that at the tobacco shop as on the newsstand where lips, breasts, and pretty legs bloom in technicolor as they do in epidermorama at the neighborhood moving picture theater, there takes shape an image of pleasure which conforms so well to the law of automatic give and take; but of a pleasure which, in order that pleasure there be, has got to occur on the spot: wham!

and it's over with, no telltale traces left behind. Just drop a coin into the slot: everything wiggles, and wiggles right! Which is illustrated by the following anecdote where those concerned are our nephew's school chums and, of course, my wife.

By various cross-checks I was able to determine that Roberte had lately, in the course of her movements about the center of town, been frequenting a women's club set up in a side street located, as if by chance, near the Lycée Condorcet, and not far from the Gare St. Lazare. This installation has some of the features of a bathing establishment and, simultaneously, of a tearoom and smacks of no telling just what sort of a meeting place for women only. Downstairs, a step or two from the washrooms—comfortable and luxurious —is gathered a team of Spanish, Italian, or Algerian shoeshine boys. When all is said and done, their presence in such a place could be considered unwarranted; and so they are only tolerated there because of their very young age and because they keep to the landing of the stairs in this basement used by other occupants in the building, which is in a commercial category. Ahead of this landing, beyond a swinging door closed by a pneumatic device, is a mirror-paneled lounge at whose farther end a second door, similar to the first, leads to the basement proper where there are bathrooms and a hairdresser's salon. From there a stairway climbs to the tearoom. Thus, if they so wish, the ladies may enter by way of the basement for their beauty care before mounting to the tearoom upstairs, or else leave the place by descending the same stairs. All the little shoe polishers or rubbers have to do is intercept a client between the two swinging doors, shove one of their shoeshine boxes under her foot and while the lady glances at herself in the mirror give this or that shoe

a dab of polish or a lick of the brush. Thus it befell that
Roberte, calling by the club one late afternoon, found herself
in this lounge. Coming from the beauty parlor—an important detail—she had on a fur coat, was putting a silk
scarf over her head, was drawing on her kid gloves. On the
steps leading down to the basement were lurking a pair of
Condorcet boys, one of whom was F., our solicitor's son, a
strapping lad of sixteen. Upon seeing Roberte, he said to his
pal, X., a little younger: "Great, she even has gloves on
today!" *

What happened then? F. and X. had bribed the little shoeshine boys and taken their place at the propitious moment,
having got the signal from the son of the building superin-
tendent, whose collaboration had been previously secured.

Roberte was about to go through the exit door when a
bellboy, carrying some greasy liquid or other in a pot, seems
to have dumped it on her shoes as he whisked past; and the
two little shoeshiners promptly spring into action, whip the
box into position, etc., etc. But I'm dubious about this detail
which looks a little to me as if it had been invented afterward to explain Roberte's amazing gesture. . . . However,
on with the story: Roberte was on the verge of going
through this final door when the two pseudo shoeshine boys
saw her pause before the mirror. Our conspirators do not
seem to have been very clever in their choice of the moment,
for if Roberte had arrived at the club with dirt on her shoes
she would have had them cleaned an hour earlier; now, she
was making ready to leave the establishment—that is why

---

* This remark is fraught with significance: Antoine's two schoolmates had made a bet with Vittorio that they would bring him
Roberte's gloves—taken from her hands, the bet hinged on that
condition.

the bellboy incident isn't altogether implausible—but the
two little shiners or rubbers saw her pause in front of a
mirror. And it was while bending toward the mirror,
amorously no doubt, that, mechanically, there's no milder
way of putting it, she planted a foot on the box. The two
little rubbers got busy and she, leaving them to do their stuff,
was at the stage of applying some lipstick when the lights
went out. Roles were shifted in a trice. X. had grabbed
Roberte's foot, posed on the box, while F., stationed behind
her, reaching his arm around in front, caught hold of the
skirt, lifted it and the bottom half of the coat and, sliding
them along Roberte's raised knee, hoisted them waist-high;
with one hand X. had immobilized Roberte's jutting leg at
the ankle and with the other he received the pocket flashlight
which F. had snapped on underneath Roberte's thigh. X.
played the beam along the smooth contours of the calf and
on up to the knee, then shot it between the garters and the
bare flesh and had got as far as the point where thigh en-
larged into buttocks poured into panties when Roberte's long
and gloved fingers settled on the bulb of the flashlight. At
that moment, Roberte, making a first effort to remove her
foot from the box, must have felt it, since she twisted around,
drawing back her hand with the intention of slapping. F.,
lifting the hem of her coat and skirt up to the small of her
back, had started by caressing her, his fingers gliding to the
crotchpiece of the panties which were stretched taut in the
wide angle between thigh and thigh, since she had one foot
on the ground and the other on the box. She was probably
planning to remove it from there by an about-face movement
with a view, if not to stop F.'s hand, already venturing into
the furthermost nooks and crannies, then at least to push
away his head which he was leaning hard against Roberte's

flank, but in front of her X. had presently taken a two-
handed grip on her calf, which forestalled this movement, F.,
from the rear, seconding his companion by blocking her
other, impatiently tensed leg, with his foot. For when
Roberte's gloved hand had closed over the bulb, X. had
quickly snatched the flashlight away and passed it to F. who
now from below directed the beam upward toward the apex
where the widely-separated thighs converged, offering X. the
rare sight of the crotchpiece that Roberte's nature was filling
out like a sail. Time enough to see that triangular yoke
billow into form and Roberte's hand grope and cover the
light a second time when, having thrust it aside, that hand
suddenly rose, Roberte then catching the beam of light
squarely in the face. While she remained thus, motionless
except for her heaving bosom, helpless under the influence
of emotion, an emotion less of surprise than of embarrassment, gasping and therefore unable to emit a sound, able
only to try to clap her gloved hand over everything F. was
illuminating, X. noticed the curve of her brow as it bent
forward, her knit eyebrows, the glint in her eyes. Maintaining the severity of her regular features, her nostrils fluttering,
her chin set firm, she was battling with both hands on the
lapels of her fur coat which F.'s adolescent fists were pulling
open, tearing her blouse, bringing the swollen brassiere out
of hiding. The very next instant, brushing past the fur, her
breasts popped forth, as if blinking in surprise to measure
themselves against unresisting, unlimited space under the
concentrated ray of electric light; the rosy, scarcely awakened
but already jaunty nipples disappeared again behind Roberte's
gloved fingers, turned up next between the schoolboy's bare
fingers—and as X., suddenly envious, clicked off the flashlight and snapped it back on in the zone delegated to him,

yet again did Roberte's hand sweep down, fingers outstretched, and X. had got a whiff of the scented skin in the
palm-opening of the glove. Just when was it that Roberte
thus reached her still gloved hand toward the treasure
bulging inside the yoke of her panties? At the very moment
they were awaiting her at the Chamber for an important
resolution bearing on the State education issue. But all notion of time and place had faded away at feeling juvenile
fingers slither purposefully under her loosened blouse, into
her armpits, over the flesh of her shoulders, toward the
straps of her brassiere, the while, lower down, her palm had
made light contact with an exceedingly youthful face, in the
darkness. Seeking a landmark, a last something real about
herself to hold onto, she placed her gloved hand upon her
groin. Actually, the young aggressor was worrying her with
an irresistible clumsiness fitting in a boy from a middle-class
family and barely in his teens, but everything the petulance
of this very lack of experience suggested of the view then
being taken of her, split her final strugglings into two contradictory solicitations: a mixture of curiosity and attentiveness containing an undeniable fervor which she had been
far from suspecting the moment before, and a more and
more dizzying uncertainty as to herself. To be sure, the
awkwardness of such untaught fingers was more crudely felt
than the hoarier articulations to whose importunings she had
been known to yield, after a show of resistance, and this
crudity, felt to the very tips of her breasts that had got away
from her own gloved fingers, strained to the snapping point
every one of the seams still holding her in between shoulders
and crotch. What was her hand doing in its glove, with this
boy she sensed behind her, squeezing her calf and pressing
his cheek to Roberte's knee so that she felt his hot breath

upon her thigh? X. indeed was breathing with ever greater
difficulty from staring, dumbstruck, at the back of that
gloved hand of Roberte's whose thumb was stiffening, index
and middle fingers lost in the folds of the yoke, ring finger
and little finger gradually separating as the middle finger,
the outline of whose nail showed through the leather of the
glove, bore into the material of the undergarment, pushing
other flesh out underneath the lace—when suddenly cloth
tore, seams gave, gloved fingers made direct contact with
the apparent bush while index and middle fingers curled
inside warm darkness, the back of the gloved hand hiding
the rest. And X., his heart beating wildly, was yet hunting
for the courage to touch that glove when, still clutching the
faultless curves of Roberte's long leg, he felt the knee suddenly buckle against his shoulder. Roberte's foot had slipped
off the box and knocked away the flashlight. A pool of light
gleamed on the enameled molding, its reflected glow shone
on Roberte's braided hair. Her eyes shut, her lips compressed
but arched by a contained laugh which was dimpling her
cheeks, with her other gloved hand she was still fending
off F.'s bare and impetuous ones teasing Roberte's nipples
inside her fur coat. Upon those naive fingers, naked and
stubby, hers, long and supple and gloved, were proving
unable to find a sure grip— when at last, having caught her
wrist, F. drew their sheath off those fingers. Denuded, the
long hand fell slack, its palm luminous. Seeing the first point
tallied by the adversary, X. could have evened the score had
he not just been smitten by that hot and rich-smelling ex-
halation from Roberte's penumbra. There lay the other hand,
still gloved in that glove which ought to have reverted to X.,
that hand which, all its fingers joined close, lay over the
thicket. But F. was brandishing the empty glove, with this

glove was lightly slapping the ungloved one's breasts: such was the force of that first tremor, so prolonged that shudder that X. thought he saw everything run out which the still gloved hand was retaining. The leather was still glistening under the light when Roberte felt her nature overflow her palm in a rush. Whereupon that hand of Roberte's he hadn't dared to unglove himself nor even touch, turned over, stretching its long fingers toward X. He, brought upright by an impulse that took him unawares, had moved only a little nearer; that gloved hand freed him slowly and surely, cleared the way for him so slowly and surely that X. could work the glove up Roberte's palm and pull in his turn: the root of the thumb appeared, and the whole of the palm's satin-smooth skin, and finally the long supple fingers which after that folded back over the boy's startled audacity, covering it with their sparkling nails. And when the root of Roberte's thumb grazed it—was it the blinding flash of the pearly nails?—X. lost sight of the reason for his pleasure while Roberte, her thighs and behind dripping with the impertinence of our two neophytes, surrendered to the last of her spasms, panting hoarsely and letting all her legislative obligations go straight to the devil, from parliamentary law-maker turning whore between Condorcet and St. Lazare. . . .

ROBERTE'S DIARY (*continued*)

"Why not permit young boys the pleasure a woman in my position would be able to procure them with disinterested sympathy and even with affection? I am coming to take a positive view of such fortuitous initiations, repugnant to me at the start: any responsible attractive woman can turn them into a real obligation—the purest and most straightforward manner of seeing to it that our youngsters avoid the very worst disasters. It isn't so much the unfortunate working-class girls I am thinking of thus saving at the same time; but also, thanks to my body, I can develop virile foundations in a good many young students, foster in them the self-assurance without which they face dreadful perplexities later on. To spare them from these at my expense is, to be sure, a 'merit' about which I need not feel called upon to boast. But when you stop to consider how some are deformed by those lamentable shifts and devices of Sodom; how others are enfeebled by the solitary practices they are driven to resort to: what distress! Remain indifferent to that stirring appeal? And how can I hesitate going to their rescue with the means I am lucky enough to have at my disposal?" That's the sort of nonsense I used to tell myself; I thought I could bring happiness to others, as if it were possible to divorce myself from a far too voluptuous giving of my person. Without providing for that thrilling experience, new to me: consenting delightedly to be paid for it. What need have I to sell myself? It's included in the rules. The fact is that many a young man's pride would have been deeply hurt had I not accepted his money. He saw that I wasn't in the profession and perhaps considered my variety of charity indiscreet. Money here confirms anonymity. What false ingenuousness; and what egoism! Even at this tender age, if not particularly then, men feel obliged to humiliate us. And I am persuaded that my being a woman in her prime, and therefore soon to be past it, is not without contributing its share to our adolescents' pleasure. Ever since I have been playing this game, what attracts me back to it despite my vague resolution to space these encounters out a little more widely is the diversity of their behavior; but above all in the four or five young men with whom I dealt last week, the extremely complicated course they shape toward pleasure; enough to lead one to believe that our children have been left more or less emasculated by the combined effects of the cinema and of the "doctrine" currently in honor at St. Germain-des-Prés. Chance brought me one gallant who, apparently inspired by the shape of the room at my former *pied-à-terre* where I had managed to take him, asked me to remain quietly seated in a chair. We are, said he, at the dentist's, in the waiting room, we wait a good half-hour and leaf through magazines, both sitting in chairs at a certain distance from each other. He then supposes that while I am twiddling my thumbs he comes up to me, the clue to his identity concealed behind his beret at first, then gradually brought far enough into the open to fluster me; I get excited. The presumption is that I pretend to go on reading a magazine, I twitch in my chair, change position, cross my legs until, still hiding my hand under a page of the periodical, I can no longer resist pulling the hem of my skirt slowly up, etc. This boy who reconstructed an obsession of his in order to satisfy it with me was just turning sixteen, was on the eve of his final exams.

OCTAVE'S JOURNAL (*continued*)

Whatever this incident's degree of probability—and I'd be only too happy to grant its entire authenticity—I am nevertheless not very pleased that it was reported as it stands to our poor Antoine; enough there to torture him for weeks, and with his examinations coming up! He thought the idea had originated with him and when they drew lots he pulled out the blank one! And F. and X. took fun in maintaining him in this cruel doubt. But there are only two culprits to shoulder the guilt in the affair: Vittorio and, eventually, Roberte. She did nothing whatsoever to disabuse Antoine. It's not this I blame her for however, but letting her admiring nephew believe that such a thing had not been impossible, she didn't give him so much as a chance to emerge from nightmare and grasp certitude . . . in an instant out of a dream: a single instant! No, come hell or high water, she clung obstinately to her role of the irreproachable tutor and at the same stroke turned the education of Antoine into the very motivation for her conduct abroad. (It wasn't until afterward I learned that obliged to justify herself before one of her superiors, she invoked this education as evidence in her favor in order to preserve her official position.) Obstinately, she was willing to have the boy suspect her of practicing what she disavowed to our faces; was prepared to refuse his schoolmates nothing, but would go on being a stone wall of purity with him, her pupil. That through my own demands with respect to Roberte I had my part in keeping Antoine in this kind of perplexity, this I'll certainly not deny. At the same time, however, I asked nothing better than to be able to make him amends. Need I say how? Roberte knew only too well what my attitude toward it would have been, and opposed to my way of looking at things to start with, she was all the more opposed to being the one to furnish it any such ratification. She knew perfectly well that Antoine had no doubt but that she conceded to others what she might have given him. And he could not understand that her antics between Condorcet and St. Lazare were for her a matter of no consequence, whereas to go to bed with Antoine at her Cité du Retiro hide-out some Thursday afternoon or simply here in the house threatened to make a shambles of her existence and of her career. This mean-spiritedness and this refusal to make a sacrifice which didn't even deserve the name of a sacrifice, that's what infuriated me, that's what turned me into Antoine's most zealous ally. How could anyone expect me not to join him in his desires when through him I felt myself grow young again and as if a second adolescence were being given to me in these my last years of life! There remains the fact that the sentimental side of the situation bothered me. Obviously, Roberte's feelings weren't very apt to be aroused by the sight of this dispirited youngster when she herself was lying under the spell of a rather more energetic presence; and while I gave my nephew some cause for hope, in so doing I omitted to show him that the nature of the things into which I had tried to push Roberte was thwarting his youthful expectations. There could, that is, be nothing less idyllic than the mood I detected in my wife. Here was a basically simple heart and I had made her ashamed of it; since, with utmost simplicity, she had contracted something which in others is the result only of a monstrous soul.

ROBERTE'S DIARY (*continued*)

In his *Roberte Ce Soir* Octave is pleased to describe me as an infallible mechanism within which my will to resist is a prisoner: my breasts and my three other organs, they and everything else function like so many parts the operator removes one by one from my control to turn them against me like my own weapons and to disintegrate me, next to put me back together again as a kind of automaton built of shame and dirt from the ground up. . . . The point of departure is that with my conjugal loyalty and my unbelief I am a monster of inconsistency. He took me for chaste. He thinks that from committing some adultery or prostituting myself I'd come to suffer in my soul and from suffering in it wind up believing it immortal, and that a salutary shame would be bred from satisfying my sensual desires; that, in short, I'd be split in two, open to grace through having opened myself to what he calls sin. This contradiction in which he would have the one half of me at loggerheads with the other, this being "driven beside myself" he expects from surrendering me to X. and Y. in the hope that thereafter I'll be unable to dispense with a "Saviour," with an "eternal and spiritual world," all that is nothing but an entirely "masculine" vision of the human being's existence that takes its start from the idea of "character"—another invention of the "male" species. We obviously haven't any "character," we aren't "the steady fulfillment of ourselves." In return how-

ever there's no beating us for pluck: we are willing to look as
if we had "character" so as to make life livable for you, to
back you up when the going gets tough—though as charac-
terless we are in our wonted and true state: as a lover very
well knows. And, my good old Octave, take this too: Vittorio, whom I'm not at all fond of, has the merit in my eyes
of allowing me to be such as I like to see myself, and that's
why anything he might happen to relate to you about me
would disappoint you: I'm made the same as all other
women, and don't need any God or Devil to say no to any
piece of dishonesty you'd like to see me commit . . . *against
myself.*

The setting, my bathroom, and the scene which unfolds
there—at nighttime (what a misapprehension!)—are inspired by the eminently masculine notion that a woman who
consents to give herself up to a lewd reverie must unfail-
ingly surrender herself to anyone who chances along while
she is in the midst of it because, lost in her dream, she lacks
the discernment necessary to turn an aggressor out of the
house as an intruder. No need to say here that no woman
who is truly a woman has ever been faced by any such alternative: if she is dreaming in such a way, she desires nobody from the outside and it stands to reason she'll brook no
nonsense from any man or for that matter from any god. If
she surrenders, it's only then she begins to dream. But dear
Octave, trying to render the alternative more plausible, presents it in a tantalizing light (men always take what excites
them to be real) for of course the woman in question is me,
now member of the National Education Commission, me,
Inspectress of Censorship. So it being I who am to let myself
go, dwelling upon the "indecent images" I'll conjure up, the
fortuitous aggressor appears at the right moment and I'm

caught: for I won't be any more able to resist him than I
was to fight off my own thoughts. There's the trap he would
have me walk into on this wonderful evening. Entrusted with
the protection of our boys' and girls' innocence, responsible
for the public's mental health, I had no reason to shut my
eyes to this filthy book, simply because my own husband was
its author; and so I have it banned. But on reaching home,
after this laudable gesture, I retire to the bathroom and then
—while, in front of the mirror, I'd be fascinated by the sight
of my own body—here's Vittorio whom my imaginings
would have inflated into this giant Pontifical Guardsman,
this Guardsman who bursts in while I am on the bidet, then
vanishes, leaving a riding crop on the floor behind him as if
in token of his invisible presence and his speedy return,
because he has just aroused me by the sight of his superb
member; there's the gesture of my hand which orders him
away although my knees are already buckling; the sudden
irruption of the horrible C. who has been spying on me to
catch me red-handed in contradiction with myself. The part
Octave relishes—he borrows this detail from an actual incident—is that I am reduced to picking up the crop, hence
that I reveal to C. that Vittorio has been here, thereby ad-
mitting his physical, tangible reality, and that renouncing
my reverie—in other words: going through to the end with
it—I acquiesce to his immediate return and consequently
agree to surrender to him; therefore already disavowing the
retributive action by which I have just publicly condemned
obscenity, ready to participate in some there and then. The
natural reaction of a woman defending herself by whatever
means she can, like hitting her aggressor—the riding crop
is nothing but a deliberately vulgar stage prop—is presented
by Octave, with incredible treachery, as an equivocal gesture

on my part. This is why when he has me lift the crop to strike C. once, a second time—C. managing to scuttle to shelter under my skirt, where he defies me then stares at me anew—Octave supposes that the blows of the crop foretell others, reserved for me in the end, and that out of this very fear I am about to strike a third time. Thereupon—and for Octave's reader this is the appropriate moment, since I am here supposed to be at the peak of exasperation—the huge Guardsman, huger than ever, materializing behind me, grabs me by the wrist, holds me fast; better still—another real detail from that incident in which I did actually get myself manhandled—the Guardsman rips off my blouse, bares my breasts and bites my shoulder so skillfully that I let go of the switch. Then the game begins, ticking along like the clockwork in a time bomb: stage by stage C. explores me from below and in front as the Pontifical Guardsman, the while fondling my breasts, undertakes to dizzy my mind by phrases cribbed from Octave's obscurantism.

The idea that "The Giant Guardsman" and "The Hunchback" are nothing else than the at first vaporous figments of my own reverie, that they take on consistency the longer I maintain my silence, becomes the device for launching a series of unspeakable scenes which from one to the next get steadily more appalling: the Guardsman enjoins me to speak, to put what he is doing to me into words; and as I persist in saying nothing my complicity increases, my resistance wanes, my senses take fire and the overly pretty Inspectress of Censorship that I am reaches a sweat at the same time of shame and of pleasure; until finally . . .

Leaving their filth aside, the design behind such elucubrations constitutes a perfect outrage to us women because it suggests the most erroneous pictures to the reader, above all to our young men, with no other view than to stimulate them to eventual enterprises which will net them the harrowing experience of being plunged into emptiness—this emptiness that our partners obstinately pursue, convinced that it is "our secret." . . . This argument of Octave's reposes on a few key ideas, in themselves much briefer and far more subtle. The gist of it all is this: on that memorable evening it was I of course who took the initiative! At all costs Octave must have me the same in my dressing room as I am at the Chamber or at the Ministry of the Interior, must have me "incarnate" Censorship, etc., from which he derives the sure-fire effects in his revolting puppet show. It never occurs to him for one instant that once I am at home, in my proper domain (the bathroom), nothing could possibly find me off guard; that if someone even as "redoubtable" but familiarly redoubtable as Vittorio were to break in on me, I remain none the less capable of greeting him with decency, decency itself being a part of the promise of a pleasure, imminent, yes, but deferred, and this especially in as much as decency is fair practice when coping with an aggressor whom you may perhaps desire all the more for cordially detesting him elsewhere than at home for other reasons. And if it happened to be an anonymous aggressor, wouldn't the temptation be greater yet? But, it goes without saying, had Vittorio actually walked in on me with that unseemly gesture, displaying to me what he displays to me in the scene my poor husband has imagined. . . . Poor Octave! Why want me such a prude when you know me to be so attractive? deny me such a natural gesture as reaching out my fingers to catch Vittorio's bird on the wing?

What Vittorio teaches me that evening is a form of pleasure that shouldn't be discussed, cannot be brought be-

fore the public eye, if a woman wishes to taste it and a man
wishes to introduce a woman to it. Whenever it comes to a
rare pleasure—*favete linguis!* That is the exact reason, the
sole reason for my hostility to your writings, my dear Octave,
and not conventional morality. Or, if you absolutely insist:
true morality serves only to safeguard the value of such
moments as those! Order, like severity, is justified by that
"interior" it shelters, that private interior—and since we
women are the everlasting guardians of these precious mys-
teries to which you men, impatient but seasoned neophytes,
want to be admitted, just give a thought to divine Augustus'
saying: "Too quickly is that achieved which is achieved for
the wishing."

Vittorio came to tell me about his worries. I consoled
him, promised him my support, and—as he then looked perfectly irresistible, exceedingly pale (oh, that olive-green hue
on a scared man's face, it's adorable!), afraid of losing his
freedom, indeed his very life, he who had threatened me not
so long ago—I steered him to what he hadn't thought would
be his that evening. He picked up immediately. Perhaps he
did put on a little apathy, at first. But what does it matter?
If he felt, as he doubtless did, a bit humiliated to have to
approach me with his problems, he had his revenge. The
surprise he gave me was the one Octave presented in his
Roberte Ce Soir, rather convincingly, as a punishment for the
woman, indispensable to the pleasure of the man; and how
can I help but declare that I felt it as a vexation. The odd
part was that Vittorio thought this the way to get even with
me for having kept him from getting his hands on little F.
during my recent outings. It could well have been that which
prevented me from fainting away while the crime was
turning into a delight. Vittorio inflicted upon me what he is

accustomed to doing to boys, worth a term at hard labor. Having removed the very loose-fitting wrapper I had put on when he arrived, he found me in my blouse, which I was still wearing, but without my skirt, and laced up in my new corset which, excellently cut, perfectly sheathed my belly and my flanks. He freed my breasts only halfway the while he was uncovering my behind and, neglecting the rest, patted and petted it very sagaciously—there being nothing about these admiring attentions I wasn't thoroughly used to . . . when up through me there ran—how am I to describe it?—a sting of amazement, from bottom to top. I bent forward, bent backward but his arms were locked around my waist. His initial attack had caused me a quick contraction but when he just as abruptly withdrew I opened myself up so blandly, with such incredible wantonness that upon feeling him become involved there a second time I squeezed, with such ease and success that my attribute filled out to the thickness of my thumb. I was dying from the wish to have him take it between his fingers, dying from fear lest it disturb him. . . .

The interest men show at such moments for this apparently "masked" attribute of ours shows how stubbornly they are bent on taking us for "shameless" creatures. They would have us be their doubles in whom what they themselves cannot have is exaggerated, and what is excessive about them they would have dwarfed in us. It isn't because we are weaker that they make us into the image of their own languor. For them a woman lying in bed half the day isn't anything scandalous at all, but instead a reassuring sign that existence can affirm itself just as triumphantly in the refusal of effort as in bustling activity. Rather, it is distasteful to them to see us, too, give signs of energy, of patience, of discernment. They are right in fearing that, out of doors, they not meet with the creatures who naturally assume what they themselves have got to leave at home in order to remain men, that is to say, in order to think, work, issue instructions, build, in short, conduct the affairs of the human race. These things they can do only provided they sense they can fall back on the permanent tepidness which emanates in successive waves from the zone we create around them. Let one of us decide—and thousands of us are doing so now—to emerge from this zone and take a hand in their tasks, they allow us to participate only upon condition they be granted occasional sips of this inertia, this emptiness they savor in us when we are inactive. If we forget to turn on this faucet every now and then we are in danger of spoiling. A woman who undertakes whatever it may be in the realm of masculine activity interests men only in so far as she is in constant risk of failing on a man's terrain, hence of missing achieving a goal she had no business setting herself in the first place. Now as soon as a woman takes it upon herself to bring something off, whether it be a cake, a dress, rearing a child, pleading in a courtroom or taking a lover, she makes a beeline for her objective, ignoring everything else and sometimes even throwing away her initial advantages. So we are owing to our innate sense of the law, of a law which renders us forever incomprehensible to men. For it is the same law which makes us into creatures alluring for their passivity and all the more delectable because this passivity too is deemed "deceitful" by our incorrigible partners, and therefore always liable for punishment; the same law which renders us unforgivable and deceiving in their eyes the moment we comply with it and are—thanks to this compliance —capable of thinking of other things besides them, of not melting under their burning kisses; a law they hate who desire nothing so much as to see us violate it. We halt awhile, periodically seconded by a gratefully indisposing "fatigue." But, resigning ourselves to it without trouble, despite our little chatterbox who simply won't keep still or go to sleep—and they count on his indiscretions!— we come out ahead here. Time works in our favor and we become inured to a seeming chilliness which guarantees us some relaxation. We venture to knit—there are so many babies being born! so many grandmothers living in ill-heated apartments!—we typewrite, we play the piano, we read— for once we have time to read!—we change our hairdo as many times as we have appointments in various places to be ready for and, on the Place Vendôme, taste the vesperal mildness of ladies' clubs in the shadow of the Ministry of Justice; we make ourselves up fit to kill, and all the same aren't at home for anybody. Nevertheless we show up when and where we are needed, she at the office of the firm she manages, she at the fashion shop or the picture gallery she has just opened, she at the counter of her tobacco shop— yes indeed, I'd have enjoyed that entertaining profession— she at her law office, at her laboratory; and she at the speaker's rostrum of the National Assembly. No man approaches us as we are about to hop out of bed, nor at lunch time. But at dinner your lover looks at you in bewilderment, declares to you that you have gone and got yourself upset over God knows what trifle, are heedless of the burning and bleeding world, impermeable, made of stone, and you listen to him rant, cigarette in your fingers, blowing a little smoke in his face when he's through. That disconcerts our partners: the peace, the complete peace reigning in us, they take it for an elaborate stratagem. The little helper is knocking off from work? Shirking under the pretense there's nothing to do? Who does she expect to fool? But what woman not utterly lost in routine has failed to notice, has failed to succumb to the advantages to be reaped from this error the male species stubbornly clings to? If need be, and your familiar neophyte is there waiting up for you when you come in at an undue hour and even finds you so lightly clad that a last-minute begging off is apt to make it seem as if you had become intractable forever, don't be afraid to lead little Tom Thumb out of the woods: it's always damp enough in there for him to look well soaked as he emerges. Pop him back in right away and let him escape a second time. If perchance he swells to about the size of your big toe, hide your face: the fable of the frog that burst from wanting to become as big as the bull does not apply to you; such boastings speak volumes, and there's a yarn your partner won't forget for a fortnight. If the little rascal stays dry withal, cover him up at once, let fly, produce a cloudburst, a tornado, as during your bona fide storms; your explorer will leave you be, fed up, proud of himself, and reassured: his weather forecasts always come true. And then go off to a night of undisturbed sleep or move on to your wholesome chores: you'll have once again given him what he was looking for—the vilest idea of yourself.

Admittedly, I'm in a pretty poor position to pass out such advice: with my too generous natural endowments, no man is likely to go away from my house otherwise than more thoroughly convinced of our inborn immodesty than ever he was before. All I can say is that in the minds of our melancholy brethren such a quality goes far beyond our physical presence. It seems that in Vittorio's view this crowning charm ought to inform my dreamy Octave better than anything I could hope to confess to him about the degree to

which I am continuously at the mercy of . . . oh, irre-
deemable innocents, everlasting schoolboys! And indeed if
a woman only acts in some male capacity, takes it upon herself to issue orders, appears holding the attributes of force
and the violent emblems of law, of justice and of charity,
comes forth a queen, a district attorney, a nurse, an air
stewardess or a gangster-girl in tights, revolver in her gloved
fist, to the masculine mind all this ostentatious or baleful
array suggests the pleasure to be derived from unmasking a
power that can at any time be shown up for what it is, hence
a voluptuous imposture that harks back to the unforgetable
detail in our physical make-up by dint of which we merit
the whip—the whip that, "ladies in boots," we brandish.
Never will men consent to fraternize with any such adversary
who attacks, encroaches upon their territory, and gets herself
bested there . . . in order to seal up the victor in his
aberration.

OCTAVE'S JOURNAL (*continued*)

What is the meaning, the purpose, of accumulating a strictly private collection of paintings which would give a legitimate joy to several people if not a crowd of them just as appreciative as I? As it happened, it was by such sheer accident. . . What's the use of this hoarding them away? With me it's not a matter of investing my money; but the refusal to contribute to the certain decline of timeless art to which the sinister "high fidelity" of spurious methods of reproduction has necessarily led already; but, above all, it pleases me to think I am withholding a given work from sight . . . the sight of someone who hasn't the right to see it? no, but of someone who, lacking the required leisure, can only be made unhappy by it; but above all of savoring the supreme pleasure of the work shining its radiance into space and recovering its own radiance therefrom—oh, unspoiled respiration, pure of the stain of even the most understanding gaze! But what would a painting be if untouched by eyes? Isn't it then that it comes to life, doesn't it die when one turns away from it, and come back to life in the next viewer? Enough; I know that argument of yours; there is nothing more living—and now desist from confusing "living" with your lamentable agitation—there is nothing more living, I tell you, than the Louvre abandoned to itself at night; of all the sensations it has so far been my lot to experience, that one was surely the most extraordinary: that confronta-

tion of paintings, that interchange, oh, purely spatial, mur-
mured between statues—what glory, comparable to nothing
unless it be the nocturnal assembly of the stars in the sky,
unless it be the Blessed Sacrament. . . . There's the "real
presence" which has no need of you. . . . And since sight
there is, the seeing can be done by a single connoisseur from
among these three million imbeciles enslaved to their social
security. Paris could perish of cold and hunger—O misguided
Abbé Pierre—and the pleasure I derive from the sight of the
"Belle Versaillaise" wouldn't be one whit impaired. The
point of view every voter is casting his ballot for nowadays,
that it would be better to dynamite the Vatican Museum, set
fire to the Louvre if that could save the lives of millions of
tots, there's one among the many posers in arithmetic this
current reproductive frenzy is producing; come on, all you
wretched curs, mop up your tears! Condemned from the
start to this incurable complaint, not only do I feel myself
"saved from the start" as you, my clerical cousin, insinuate,
but at birth I acquired the right to inalienable spitefulness;
that's my orthodoxy. . . . Fiddlesticks, were you to hear
the moans of a child suffering from meningitis, of a soldier
undergoing an amputation without anesthesia, were you to
see a young person disfigured by some horrible disease, you'd
stop at nothing to save them if saved they could be. —Why
of course, it's only too true! This fearful weakness caused
in us by the gaping wound in our originally intact soul, by
this even more appalling cancer you call responsibility, this
breach through which the screams of these victims beyond
number pour flooding into us, this typhoon which blasts our
insides empty, which undermines our foundations, causes us
to lose our balance on this so narrow platform being has
contrived for our ventured self—for we are only "ventured"

before becoming "venturing"—who then, if only he could, wouldn't plug up this breach and live like a monster, monstrously serene, immune to pity? If this isn't so, then happiness is nothing but horror, which is just what you imply, sinister tale-bearers that you are, tune-callers of woe who have based your shameless reputation upon the throbbings of that wound, upon the irritations you provoke there as you cunningly turn the knife in it. Horror of happiness? Horror of life which you are now in the unqualifiable habit of trampling upon since it has become for you the synonym of injustice, of scandal, of atrocity. You wouldn't be able to sleep in peace the day there weren't any torturers, murderers, exterminations to denounce—and the day all that were to happen in our streets, in our houses, in our bedrooms, I know more than one individual who'd jump on a plane for Venezuela. And I? —What would you do, Octave old boy? Ah, your kindly disposition would get the better of you, wouldn't it, you'd turn your wife over to the Asiatic like the nasty coward you are and sitting in your wheelchair you'd die watching her disgrace before they came to shoot you. But between now and then . . . —As long as there's a "between now and then" get the hell out of here and take that plane today. Happiness is either blindness or happiness there is none. And you, Cousin Canon, your final bliss doesn't exist unless it is blindness too. For if it isn't, it won't escape the echo of the gnashing of teeth rising up from the underworld; which is why your own John XXII denied that the sight of blessedness could begin before this world disappears. But to pack the blessed into a stadium while in the smoking and bottomless arena below sinners, male and female, gesticulate, squirm, cavort, as Doctor Angélique suggests—really, I can't help preferring my Louvre, since without knowledge of all the miseries there is no reason why the sight of blessedness thus conceived cannot begin there! As for you others, spreaders of news of woe, hired poisoners of our instants of fortune, do something useful for once, such as campaign for a ten-year suspension of births. My soul is cramped for space, for air, it spoils, and things have got to the point where only yesterday I treated myself to a *tableau vivant,* a lively one, and for it paid a pretty sum which thereby went to no family of refugees. . . . Oh, these refugees, they were . . . no, honestly now, hasn't D.D.T. been invented? And to think, old Philippe, that those troublemakers got the better of you! Ah, the strange beauty of that period when the Teuton so stupidly did us a favor: you could walk in peace along the river bank crowded with nothing but the finest memories, you rediscovered Paris, and the trees got back their native strength and gracefulness as though waking up from a long hibernation, from the long winter of the infamous Third Republic, swaying in the sweet illusion of the Monarchy restored. . . . My nose drips, my tears run into my long mustaches, and the grime on my body is only the mourning I wear in honor of that golden opportunity which faded away. Do you remember, Philippe, our plan was to bring back its royal aspect of olden times, if not to the whole of France, at least to Greater Paris. To that end, no more factories and, at the same stroke, no more Red Belt. Let the Jerries cart everything away, and ship them as many people as possible into the bargain, clear France of her restless elements, get rid of everybody except the women and children, watch Germany gorge herself on manpower and eventually choke from her industrial crises, her riots, and finally rot under Moscow's thumb. The longer the war lasted, the more time we'd have had to do a thorough and thoughtful house cleaning. We'd auction North Africa and Indochina off to the highest bidder and, sitting tight behind our foreign exchange reserves, we'd tuck ourselves into our little revival of Syagrius' kingdom. It was plain common sense: with a wisely trimmed, carefully controlled density of population we'd return to an artisan civilization, a civilization based on manual skills—heh, all sorts of manual skills. The gates of Paris would be shut, first of all to put a stop to the rural migration toward the capital: keep the peasant-folk down on the farm, tied to the good earth, and get that sturdy, thrifty race of Auvergne yeomen to increase tenfold, Auvergnats in every province. The impossibility of finding employment in Paris, where only those families settled there for a minimum of seventy-five years would be authorized to reside! The young men sparse in the population, but women and girls in abundance, and lots of old men! No high public office for anyone under forty-five. Hence no retirements! Large families nowhere except among the economically handicapped at best. A well-organized, sustained, clean lower class benefiting from modest living conditions, poor and honest, a dwindled proletariat destined to disappear with the last of the factories. As for Paris, transformed back into a middle-class town of sedentary Parisians coming from sound old stock, there'd be nothing but libraries, museums, and entertainment. . . . Finally, nothing but a Senate named by family heads sixty years old and over. Our graybeards, for the past hundred years at least, our graybeards have always been the salvation of this country, our petulant youth have ruined it. In France they have constantly been sowing a wind, producing wind alone. For the Teuton, the Slav, to seek his destiny in storm and stress; the style becomes him, though the Teuton seems tired of it at last. As for us, we must first become embittered to become tougher, more leathery, more taciturn but above all more tight-fisted than we are. With us it isn't generosity which proves creative in social life: to the contrary, it has always been sheer waste, and no work prompted by generosity has endured. But the mistrust, the slander, the delation, the cold-blooded wickedness which derives from the sternly impassive spirit, that's the stuff that used to make us grow up into an inviolable contempt for our fellow man! Only in the frosts of old age do such virtues come to flower, for with many among us beneath that ice lurks fire. To teach young men that nothing is so important as to prepare for their old age, the finest period in life if one can reach it—remain sober, continent—this is the sense in which priests are useful, up until the fifties. But then with all that pent-up vitality, all the hoarded sperm as well as all the hoarded money, borne high by the decline of one's years, to enjoy the golden sunset of life—that, it seems to me, is as much as we can hope for in this corner of the world, one of the richest in treasures. Such is the view of our last great painters: they fixed forever the image of a life doomed to disappear.

ROBERTE'S DIARY (*continued*)

"If I altogether let myself go there would be more coveting in the glances I cast upon my nephew's dawning manhood. But the price I'd have to pay in doing so would be the immediate withdrawal of my affection for him. I have none for little F. or little X. of whom he may have some reason to be jealous. It cannot be said that I endured their insolence without obvious emotion, and I had all I could do not to leave traces of it on their inky, artless fingers. But for Antoine who knows more or less nothing about it, it's that much the better: two years from now he'll only look back with a smile, with embarrassment, on the little sorrows I am causing him for the greater good of his stability—and some pretty young thing will attend to the rest."

That is what I'd always thought . . . until very recently when I fell into the ambush the old devil set for me. Now what's going to happen? Antoine cannot possibly have understood, it's impossible that he not be made sick at the stomach by the recollection of my garden into which he stumbled thanks to that pious rake. Roberte, nothing but a sink of iniquity, that's what he must think, a cesspool . . . You can't get away with offending a boy's sense of smell, not when he's that young. . . . I . . . what did I do? What was I after? Cure him of the exalted picture he had of me, physically I mean? And why that abrupt decision, that sudden impatience on my part? That destruction in one fleeting instant of everything I had cultivated, built up with as much joy as effort? Why have ruined myself in his eyes when there was nobody else at hand to replace me forthwith? Then by what was I guided? Has Octave after all rendered me so docile to his foul visions that I rush straight into the picture he is now amusing himself painting? Am I enthralled to the point where I'm led to sacrifice my nephew's innocence, sacrifice, with my own hands, the very thing upon which my freedom was based? But isn't it true that I loathe this husband of mine, this unclean voyeur? Or have I come to the pass of living according to yesterday's truths only because they'll be lies tomorrow? Would it be true, Roberte, that you need him, this evil old man oozing vice, that you love him for his flattering ignominies?

I bury my face in my hands. My thoughts come to a stop and the scent of my hands begins to make my head reel. Alas, I am in love with my own self; yes, my hands have an added reality for me now that they are no longer able to protect a vulnerable innocence, my hands which are unable to protect me anymore, my too beautiful hands which are meant only for the occasions that arise from my defeats. Antoine saw them at work: may they at least have given him more than the pleasure he looked forward to getting from them, the desire to renew it—for, Roberte, as regards the proof of that pleasure, your hands were steeped in it. . . . And now how am I to put him on the right road? I invoke some nameless and forgotten religion which might give me the certitude of having in all this observed some great eternal law that towers mightily over me and sanctifies me. Sanctifies? I rave. . . . Well, what else . . . ? To be called a slut, as Vittorio did in the presence of my nephew, is an enormous comfort to me. And so here I am, behold, the faithful wife of the most loathsome of husbands; unworthy aunt of the most charming of nephews. And, here, even as I spell out the word "charming," I cannot write it without having the juvenile petulance of his developing body forced upon me. . . . Buck up, Roberte, show your natural kindliness, as that hilarious Octave would say, and let's take the scene through once again. . . . I wept, I wept terribly afterward, but the family honor called for it. A woman stooping that low in front of her nephew. Am I going to start to cry again? The milk is spilled. "The best thing, alas, would be to do it again, right this time," and that was all my godfather G. had to say to me this morning when I went to cry on his shoulder because of all that. Do it again—with more decency, less affectation, but do it again—right. My thighs have slipped apart . . . while I apply myself to my writing like the young deaconness I was fifteen years ago. It's four o'clock, they're expecting me at the Chamber—the one nausea distracts me from the other.

OCTAVE'S JOURNAL (*continued*)

(Continuation of the Descriptive Catalogue to my Collection)
"La Belle Versaillaise"

Below the high arcades of the rue de Rivoli whose retreat into the distance forms the background of the painting—far off, the Palais des Tuileries is in flames—three large figures dominate the foreground: a lady flanked by two men. The lady, young, elegant, wearing a broad-brimmed hat, being pushed by one of the two fellows—they are Communards—pulled by the other, almost an adolescent. The man on the right, burly, wearing a peaked cap, is brandishing the parasol he has wrested from the young woman and with which he is about to hit her, thrusting his free hand into her tattered bodice and catching a handful of one of her bared breasts. Indeed, her skirt probably lost in the course of a preliminary mauling, for she is in lace-fringed pantaloons, the young woman's legs, sheathed in smooth dark-gray stockings, show her poised to make a dash; the left leg slightly bent, the foot striking the ground with the heel of her shoe, the right leg, knee raised high, forming a right angle, the entirely bare thigh in profile contrasting with the silk-sheathed calf. The bust is shown in three-quarter view, the head carried high, the face turned toward the aggressor on the right; her brows knit in a frown below the slightly turned-down brim of the jonquil-yellow hat. The

gaze of her fine gray eyes, indignant and questioning, the
straight nose, the full cheeks, the equally contemptuous and
graceful arch of her lips, the face pale except for the faintly
flushed cheeks, the rounded chin completing the perfect
oval of this face whose lower part is just above the shoulder
of the naked arm stretched out horizontally and thus ex-
posing the reddish-brown hollow of the armpit and all the
breast that starts out of the unlaced bodice. The left forearm
raised but sharply twisted—the young man having seized it
with both hands—the right arm lifted also but bent at the
elbow, the forearm pointing upward but the gloved hand
turned so as to show the palm whose flesh appears in the
opening of the glove, the fingers curled in toward the hollow
of the hand, the thumb pressed against the index finger,
expressing futile resistance, while the left hand, shown with
its back facing us, all its fingers outstretched, describes a gesture of terror wherein the pathetic yields to provocation. The
bull-necked adolescent, coatless, his torso straining backward
but his head lunged forward, disheveled, wild-eyed, grinning,
his lips twisted boastfully, draws the lady to him with his
muscular arms, bracing a foot against the curb edging the
wall back of him, the other leg thrust forward, ready to
catch the lady who, as she falls, with her lifted knee is stag-
ing a last defense. While the aggressor on the right, despite
the hand he has reached into the bodice, seems impelled not
so much by desire as by the vulgar satisfaction of thrashing
a fashionable lady; an extreme impatience, a brutish eagerness for the pleasure which the circumstance holds forth to
him animates the youth whose thick butcher-boy's fists, their
ruddy tint contrasting with the fair one's gloved hands, have
gripped her wrist so securely. And indeed such magnificent
hands, the one with its long fingers extended, the other with

them closed tight, had necessarily to be painted wearing leather gloves; here the artist's subtlety was to show this nudity of alabaster arms, this ocher tint of the thighs, particularly of the lifted thigh, these mauve and blue tones of the already rumpled pantaloons, all the while leaving our imagination to visualize the skin of these lovely hands, their suppleness and tenseness underneath such dark-gray gloves. The fair lady of Versailles' breast, her belly are already exposed, surrendered, her secret charms are certain to be very soon, and to conceal her feelings she has nothing left but her gloves: the symbol of the distance she wished to put between herself and the gaze of others, this precaution against sullying contacts only contributes to heighten her social downfall and at the same time that of a conventional modesty. If the straightened fingers express panic, the hand with the fingers clenched to the palm whose surface emerges in the glove-opening bears witness to shameful sensations. And although the physiological effects of such emotions do not readily lend themselves to pictorial description, the fact remains that the manner in which the artist chose to treat this detail is not without a suggestive force I'd dislike having to refrain from mentioning, bowing to the idea that it is unhealthy and, after all, of no interest from the technical point of view. After all, it's by means of nothing else than his craftsmanship that the artist undertakes to make me feel that in his haste, the young man won't even bother to unglove those superb hands; that, sure of his quarry, he'll be less concerned to avenge his comrades than to vent upon her the violent desires she excites in him. Little does it matter whether, guilty or not of some of the atrocities committed by women upon Communard prisoners, the lady experiences as punishment or as outrage that which the butcher-boy is

dead certain to wreak upon her. If I am told that I'm indulging in tattletales, that I'm dreaming out loud, I'll draw the
tough-minded connoisseur's attention to the conspicuous relationship established between the mimicry of the hands and
the treatment of the lady's face. One has simply to observe
the finished execution of these elements—from the ivory tone
of the palm appearing through the glove-opening, the bent
fingers, the impress of the fingernail upon the leather, to
the stitches on the back of the glove—in order to understand
the function of these details in this upper part of the painting where, on a level with the hat whose brim drawn down
toward the eyes adds to the coquetry of the indignant glance,
these gloved hands are of such importance in relation to the
whole. The overall impression is one of the feminine body
dressed, fully decked out, hidden, but revealed at its extremi-
ties—hat, make-up, gloves at the top, shoes, silk stockings
at the bottom—whereas the unveiled middle part anticipates
the moment of impending violent possession. For the rib-
boned hat, the suede gloves, the filmy lace-trimmed undergarment, the farthingale dress once lost, harmonized with
the lofty architecture of the rue de Rivoli arcades; but the
Tuileries tumbling in flames, the frantic prancing of the
high-heeled shoes, the glossy tension of the stockinged legs,
this frightened separation of the thighs spreading within
anger-charged space, these warm tones gleaming upon the
surface of this belly offered to the rabble are evidence of
burns caused by a subtler fire: so many aspects of the incident which wouldn't have had their impact either upon the
aggressors or upon a chance witness to it, which would have
been registered by no one except the young woman undergoing the experience. Is one to believe that in depicting the
ruin of her social vanity the artist may have ascribed to her

as much premeditation in her gestures as he himself has employed upon this painting, or else has he revenged himself in showing her swept away by the animality of her own reflexes? May he have composed the unfurling of an act of seduction? Is this offering us an object for contemplation which insures the tranquillity of our spirit? And is not the painter's noblest function to procure us a remorseless quietude? Is there not risk enough that my own description, though based on the painting's material reality, hints at a morbid reverie? Tonnerre may have dreamed in a similar way, but he subjected his intimate ghosts to the rigors of his art. The result being that he justified and liberated himself, although he more than once started in again. Tonnerre dead, practically unknown, his unexhibitable picture has afforded me more than one reprehensible quarter of an hour. If I expose it, I gain him a doubtful celebrity. If I keep it closely to myself, the words his painting suggests to me will go on striving to turn me into the stunned witness of this possible and awful incident. But each time I fall wide of the mark, in the impalpable region that is less created than dug in my mind by these fiery words, lashed, torn out of me in this evening of my life: "La Belle Versaillaise" . . . Be that as it may, I wholeheartedly applaud the wise severity of our guardians of law and order, I applaud their concern to withhold any such plastic exhibition from the sight of the young, above all from the sight of the crowd! leaving discriminating art-lovers to reserve exclusive rights to what they enjoy.

ROBERTE'S DIARY (*continued*)

This day ends for me on the borderline between delirium and shame: it is more than I can do to continue to live in the obsessive consciousness of such a failure, put at my wits' end by physical sensations which are rendering me unrecognizable to my own self. Neither can I simply get a separation from Octave—a great quibbler, as everybody knows—without having both sides of the family up in arms. There'd remain the last, the inconceivable resort . . . hasten his end. Let's at least give some calm thought to this solution, mad though it may appear (and then perhaps tear out this page once it has been written, for, to get it out of my mind, it has got to be set down in black and white): finish off Octave, slowly, quietly, surely—the state he is already in makes the thing so easy, no suspicion could be aroused: render him still more senile than he is now. The obvious ease with which I might have stooped to such a thing probably explains why it never occurred to me, when I could have done it so legitimately! But . . . wouldn't something like this be completely in his style? Ah, I am still too fond of my shame to be able to escape it by means of this naive gesture. If at present I wish for his death it's because, his task achieved, he is most needlessly outliving his day and preventing me from finally living as he always wanted me to. And afterward? I'll still be able to take Antoine in hand: I'll make use of his passion, I'll satisfy it with greater certainty, afterward; I'll send him off to a better start in life. And I'll feel myself strengthened for having converted into a triumph something which up until then was no more than an illusion that had been doing him damage. . . .

OCTAVE'S JOURNAL (*end*)

(Final Notes Dictated on his Deathbed to Vittorio)

A strange *tableau vivant,* this that was presented to me in celebration of my seventieth birthday: *The Fair One Has Herself Surprised While Poisoning Her Drowsy Old Husband.* A "wooer" whose assiduities she rejected in favor of another appears just as she has finished administering the contents of the fatal cup which she, at her victim's bedside, is still holding in her hand. Stupefied, she is rooted to the spot, sweating infamy and shame, while the redoubtable witness, menacing her with an immediate denunciation, bares her rump and, altogether at his ease, beneath her admirable buttocks prepares the avenues of twofold vengeance. Ordered by him to do so, she keeps the cup in her hand, her thumb and forefinger joined on its foot, her palm at the mercy of the "poisoned" party (me). This latter, his eyes half-closed, watches the quiverings of the criminal and voluptuous hand as the thrill heralding the penalty she is about to undergo is gradually communicated to her fingers and to her fingernails' flashing knavery. And sure enough, the "wooer" (Vittorio), with one hand lifting her dress and petticoat, signals to a youthful personage clad in scarlet, and masked; the executioner approaches. Roberte, in the role of the poisoner-adulteress, notwithstanding her willingness to play her part in the *tableau vivant* game, seems to have no idea of the identity of the younger of the two disguised individuals. And thus are my suspicions confirmed *in extremis:* she imagines that she has me too thoroughly in the dark by now to be able to realize Vittorio's presence here, and that I know nothing at all about her informal relations with little F. She thinks it is with him she is dealing underneath that costume whereas he who is wearing it is no other than her own nephew. What I am in fact witnessing is Antoine's revenge, and the pathetic quality of the character he is impersonating is wonderfully suiting to the resentment stirring him and with which he is already touching the punishable parts of the "poisoner." In his lucid agony, the "poisoned" husband sees, with one eye, the fair hand lose its grip on the empty cup; suddenly seized by wild laughter in her proper role, Roberte has straightened out her fingers, laid them over my eyelids and, pressing her palm against my lips, by the furious scream that rings out from the middle of her dumb show informs me that justice has been done. . . . Ah, between her spread slender fingers I was able to see nevertheless, I still see, I shall always see . . .

What? Somebody at the door? The Canon . . . ? Under no circumstances . . . All's already forgiven . . . Tell him that "*All heaven rejoices* . . . "

ROBERTE'S DIARY (*continued*)

Peace at last. But, is it to be believed? Octave was summoned away by his God. Oh, what rescuing miracle could ever bring more heartfelt, more cheerful offerings of thanks from me? My God, if despite all the facts you do exist, you have saved me from the final blunder that would have spoiled everything; and as my father the pastor would remind us at such a moment, it is written that "Thou shalt not be tempted unto that which thou hast not the strength to do" . . . But if I am nevertheless unable to believe in the Supreme Judge it is even harder for me to believe in Octave's death: from beyond the grave he is watching me. Am I then going to remain his ballet dancer forever? Am I to lend myself to posthumously staged productions, strain to hear his applause? Or else is it the disappearing of his gaze that suddenly catches me unprepared? I find myself alone, restored to myself, and there shall be no more of that unending commentary upon my gestures, my movements. That dreaded glance cast into my affairs—there's something even more to be feared henceforth. Antoine freely awaits only one thing which I am called upon to freely satisfy— and now that life is no longer a play on a stage life begins anew, but in a serious vein, with still greater seriousness now that the task at hand is to school a lover.

But since life has to be resumed, let me look for that bend in the road where I parted company with the person I was ten years ago. . . .

ROBERTE'S DIARY (*end*)

(Continuation and Conclusion of
The Roman Impressions)

Nec dolent prava,
sed frustra voluisse.
—Seneca

Finding myself in Rome on the eve of the Allies' entry into the city, I in my capacity of a volunteer attached to the Swedish Red Cross went through experiences as strange as any ever to have befallen a girl who has always lived in strict accordance to her Calvinist beliefs and who sees the principles of her religion put to the test. My father, Pastor J., had approved my interrupting my law studies in order to join the convoy of doctors and nurses being assembled in Geneva, where I spent the month of August in 1943. And thanks to my uncle, Professor B. of the Faculty of Medicine in Geneva, I, though a French citizen, had no trouble getting to the Eternal City, still in Kesselring's hands when I landed there. Mussolini's fall, the setting up of the Badoglio government, the struggle between the Italian administration and the camouflaged residues of the Fascist police and the Gestapo, the sensational kidnaping of Mussolini by that Z., the Hungarian paratrooper—so many incidents which in neutral diplomatic circles enlivened the small talk at dozens of cocktail parties held during the last air raids. A good many

people, not only Italians and Germans but also of Balkan
origin and naturally some stray Englishmen and Frenchmen
too, would try to crash our get-togethers, eager to draw a
smoke screen over the undefinable functions they had exer-
cised under the regime of oppression, and would angle for
odd jobs, anything that would look well on their record in
case the Anglo-American police subsequently got on their
trail. We alone, along with the neutral diplomats, had access
to the Vatican and the most charming Monsignors were always on hand to facilitate our mission. Two famous convents
turned over their annexes while we were still waiting for
suitable space to be prepared in the hospitals already jammed
with prisoners and serious cases. Now, side by side with this
activity, I found myself engaged in some other very delicate
business involving the recuperation of Jewish children who
had been dispersed among various religious congregations
through the agency of the Roman clergy; it must have been
a pell-mell sort of operation, and it was only a while later
that I realized it hadn't been solely to preserve them from
persecution that their birth certificates had been altered. . . .

But before telling you how I managed to accomplish my
task I'd like to say something of my own state of mind
during those unforgettable weeks. . . . Amidst such a sea
of agitation and anxiety, within the superb setting of this
city which has known so many disturbed periods since its
beginnings, in apprehension of the dramatic hours in which
its deliverance would transpire and with that feeling of snug
well-being under the wing of guardian angels protecting us
in the middle of general insecurity, in spite of a thousand
and one trying details I was taking a curious liking to the
scene, I felt the pulse of life quicken in me: the contact with
wounded soldiers, the care I lavished upon them, the unfail-

ing attention my charms aroused from the superficially
wounded and, despite an initial repugnance only too swiftly
surmounted, the caresses I did not restrain myself from giving now to one, now to another, a mixture of teasing and
of a budding maternal affection in the agreeable pleasure
caused me by the only too short-lived relief I procured them
—this exceedingly winning German parachutist, an over-
grown boy still in his teens who played soulful tunes on his
harmonica, or again that impish little dark-eyed Sicilian who
notwithstanding his hideous wound would give me gracious
smiles from his warmly modeled lips. . . . Wouldn't such
surroundings provide any young woman an excuse for going
just a bit berserk in one way or another, would any free
young woman be able to resist?

The military hospital I was supposed to visit every day
was installed in a palace formerly belonging to the Princes
of V., and had gardens all around it. Once past the cordon
of sentinels you walked under the archway of a magnificent
portal set in a vestibule of tall columns. From there rose a
broad stairway with marble balustrades, flanked by statues
and busts; I climbed it every day between moving lines of
prisoners, nurses, orderlies, military policemen milling in
groups on the stairs, an indescribable confusion revealing
the general nervousness before the imminent arrival of the
Allied armies. On the first floor, by way of a pair of double
doors, wonderfully sculptured but with their panels knocked
out and replaced by panes of glass, you entered a reception
hall for the time being divided into various compartments
where the sick and wounded were placed according to the
gravity of the case. That is where I spent a part of my after-
noons, there that I found the little Sicilian and many other
boys with whom I became familiar. The Italian medical

officer on duty that day—the Allied troops were expected in Rome at any moment—asked me to keep an eye on the behavior of a wounded German who had just been through a lengthy and wearing examination. I had noticed him before during previous visits, but as I had been accompanied I'd only given him a brief and entirely well-mannered smile; enough however to make Louise, our supervisor, bristle. A high-ranking officer, S.S., so it was said, there was nothing about his looks that would put you off; heavens, no, a handsome fellow of thirty to forty at the most. Alone, running no risk of being observed by my importuning and talkative companions, I went and sat down by his cot. He was bundled up in his blanket and seemed to be taking a nap. With my handkerchief I dried the drops of sweat on his brow and spontaneously touched my fingers to it. I watched my nails glisten in this fine-looking man's curly hair and felt just like a damosel in medieval times comforting her knight errant —when I was snatched out of this start of a daydream by a lively dispute that arose between two medical officers and the sentry of the ward. One of the two doctors, a German, was complaining to his Italian colleague that he couldn't find a trace of a wounded man he had operated on the week before. "The regulations have changed since your people left," the Italian declared. "Yes, and what a God-awful mess things are in, what a mess!" the German retorted. Meanwhile Von A.—but I didn't learn his name until afterward, the temperature-chart on the wall only mentioned the seriously wounded patient's serial number—Von A. had awakened. He had probably heard the indignant exclamations uttered in his native tongue—but, as I went back to gazing at him, he spoke to me, his eyelids half-raised, saying in the very best French: "Some more, would you, some more, your cool pure hand is soothing. . . ." The German medical officer walked by at that same moment, casting distraught glances to left and right, stopped at the foot of Von A.'s bed and seeing that he was almost asleep, looked at me and nodded politely. "Excuse me, Schwester, has he been here for only a few days?" "No," I replied, "for a month." He turned away and I was already up, meaning to offer to help him find the person he was searching for, when I felt arms thrown around my waist. I turned and sank down on the handsome officer's bed: "Schwester," he whispered, hitching himself up with a painful effort, "Schwester, I don't want to finish this way. . . . They lied to us, I myself lied to others, we're worse than cannibals. . . . I want to be regenerated . . . you could make a new man out of me. I won't ever see Malwyda again. . . . You resemble Malwyda, oh, you look so much like her!" and more and more breathlessly: "and the children Malwyda would have given me! Why not give me children as Malwyda would have done!" This torrent of self-accusation, this gush of sentimentality in the wounded man terrified me. Truly, this outdid any of my previous experiences.

Contriving to master my embarrassment, "Malwyda," I asked, "she's your . . . fiancée?" and after that rather foolish question I busied myself arranging his pillow so as to keep up my appearance of casualness. But he was staring at me with his intensely blue eyes: "Malwyda! Fiancée! Me get engaged when I had Malwyda? She's my sister! How could you want to have children by anyone else than your own sister? Tall, beautiful . . . serious-faced, like you!" "You see, you aren't completely awake. . . . Go back to sleepy-bye. . . ." It was one of the dodges Louise used to get out of ticklish situations, and I now tried it to escape this deluge of confidences. "I'm not Malwyda! Would you like me to have a message got through to her?" He seemed to be musing. "I don't know where she is at the moment. She must have left Hamburg," and he made a weary gesture with his hand. Then, staring at me: "But you're here. . . . You're here and you never come to see me. It's . . . being very dignified . . . yes, I understand." "Now just look," I said, not without an impudence altogether excusable in the idiot I then was, "everything happens if you wait long enough: today I'm here!" And so saying, my hands folded in my lap, I crossed my legs, one calf over the other and well in evidence. He gazed at me, a hint of bitterness in his smile; after a little he frowned and in a more sober tone said, "You could do me a favor," and began to fumble in his jacket, hanging on a hook by his bed. From inside he unfastened a little cross. When he had it loose I noticed that it was soldered to the end of an iron key, hand-wrought and seemingly old. "You might do me a favor," he went on and then, interrupting himself, a scared expression coming over his face, "no, it's not possible," and he fell back on his cot. "What is this key? And why should it be impossible?" "This key opens . . . a tabernacle." "What?" "Yes, Schwester, it's the key to the tabernacle in a little chapel. That's where I put Malwyda's letters before I went to Anzio." "What an idea . . . How could you have . . ." He declared that had he kept them on his person and been killed, these letters might well have been sent back to the family and a dreadful scandal would have ensued. That in this inviolable place they were better than just safe. Disconcerting, all this, for either he was still speaking from within a delirium as he had seemed to have been a while ago, or else, if he was lucid and telling the truth to me, to me whom he didn't really know at all, what was the object of so many mysterious precautions? Unable to make out just where fairy tale ended and sincerity began, I felt obliged to take him at his word, and ventured: "Why exactly in a tabernacle?" for nothing was more unpleasant to me than the idea of this accessory of the Roman rite. He at once gave me an even more baffling reply: the contact of these letters with the Holy Sacrament could have an influence upon his relations with his sister. Then, right away, he asked if I weren't a Catholic too, and as I raised both hands and backed off from the conjecture, identifying myself as the daughter and great-granddaughter of Calvinist ministers, he remarked that his gesture probably made no sense to me at all since "the real presence" didn't exist for us others. I was wary of informing him of the inexistence of such a dogma for me and, refusing to enter into a debate of this kind, I limited myself to saying that a tabernacle was in no way inviolable—that, furthermore, the fact he had the key to one such pretendedly sacred piece of furniture proved it. Who'd given it to him? He asserted that it had been turned over to him by the Italian chaplain at his headquarters in Rome, and as I didn't appear at all convinced, he added that the Germans had shot that priest as a spy—and ended his explanation there. To this I deemed it best to say nothing, and I affected a certain reserve; but he was quick to draw me out of it and, catching hold of my hand, wanted to know if I had any objection to going and removing those letters for him from the place where they were presently deposited. "I?" said I, pretending surprise even though I was doubtful about the whole business. But he sought to persuade me that I now being the only one who knew what he had just told me, only I could enter such a place and do such a thing since, as well, I did not, deep down within me, think I had anything to fear from the real presence. To be sure, he had guessed right, but to test the truth of his story I advised him to hand this key over to the hospital chaplain who would be coming by in a short while. "Ah no, most certainly not," said he, "I haven't any confidence in these priests around here: nothing but a gang of spies!" And he stuck the key under his pillow.

And then I became perplexed. Something indomitable and somber now froze the face of this handsome chap who had seemed so easy to take in charge as he lay dozing. I need hardly note here that I have never had any instinctive sense for what would distinguish an enemy from another man; with its branches spread throughout various countries in Europe, my family has for centuries had no enemy other than the Papacy, no homeland other than Freedom of Conscience. Ever since the Revocation of the Edict of Nantes, Protestant freedom, so I assumed, was as good as barred from life; Rome had won out on a good many scores, not at all, mind you, that Rome was the Church, but because life defied the condemnation the Evangile hurled at Rome. And, carrying the faculty for free inquiry to the point of absurdity, I had opted for that defiance, not so much from love for life as to assert what I then took to be my freedom. Consequently, all the rest—why these nations were fighting at the moment, in the name of what humane and pleasant ways of life and thinking against other deliberately atrocious ones—everything led back to this freedom to choose for or against life. By what right could you deny it to others, even if their choice might be in favor of the very worst—that's what I wasn't able to understand. But was I only trying to understand? Charity came to my rescue: no more problems! Go join the Red Cross: as if tending to the blind, you'll tend indiscriminately to them who know not what they do, the "guilty" and the "innocent" alike. What was the war to me? A tumultuous facet of life: a lot of boys assembled whose fate was to beat, to pillage, to burn, it didn't much matter for the sake of what, we women were there to care for them, nurse them, calm them, distract them; thus had it always been before, so it would be ever after! And here was the war, which as a woman I thought I could foil by means of the fortuitous incidents that composed it, such as this meeting with Von A., the war was forcing its most awful aspect upon me: the consciousness of duty! If indeed this key really did belong to a tabernacle and if this tabernacle did contain some secret documents, elementary loyalty demanded that I myself reveal the affair to the hospital chaplain. And doing that went terribly against the grain. What need had I to bring the outside world into this pattern of coincidences which stemmed so naturally from my own initiative? My thoughts were at that stage when, height of bad luck, I saw the unbearable Louise arrive. Lean, hollow-eyed from all-night vigils, she was a perfect specimen of the toughened old maid, seasoned, proud of the sacrifice of her four nephews slaughtered on miscellaneous fronts. Austerity, bereavement, courage, and resignation were all incarnated in her single skinny person, the living denial of all joys, permissible as well as forbidden; in short, the final crushing argument which reduced me to silence. So I loathed her. As soon as she spotted me beside Von A.'s bed she waved at me impatiently. Slowly, as slowly as possible, I got up, casting a glance at Von A. But he, having recognized her too, and at the mere sight, had promptly rolled over toward the wall, which put the crowning touch on my bad mood. When I went up to Louise she had her hand on her hip: "Keep away from the ones in that category, little girl, they aren't in your line. Those are orders." "You haven't got any orders to give me," I answered back, looking at the rows of decorations brightening her flat chest, "I'm not a professional, I'm a volunteer. . . ." "Leaving your impertinence aside for the moment—and we'll have some more to say about it later— just respect discipline and do as you're told." "Ask the Italian medical officer if he didn't ask me to stand by over here." "Okay Roberte, I'm taking you off duty. Go back to quarters. Shoo." Whereupon I slipped out of the ward, firmly intending to return when Louise had finished her own inspection, that day limited to finding out how her pet was coming along: a plump little horror of a traveling salesman from Bordeaux who had enlisted in the L.V.F., been hit somewhere in an air raid while en route for Austria, and had ended up at Rome instead of on the Russian front. I had the time to saunter down the big stairway and feast my eyes on two superb adolescents in black shirts, orderlies, I believe, and to rebuke myself for having been so sharp with poor Louise. How she'd have gloated had she happened upon me while I was staring at those two boys! Finally seeing her emerge in the company of the medical officer, I ducked behind one of the statues on the ramp—a copy of Donatello's young David—and admiring its delicately jointed limbs, I absent-mindedly ran a finger down the curves of its leg. Ahead of me, two Bersaglieri were peering at me, probably surprised to see a nurse standing about idle too; they exchanged winks, one turned in my direction: "Looking for somebody, Signorina?" "No," I said, "no, I think I must have taken the wrong stairway," and I flew up the steps and back into the ward. Beaming, I sat down beside my knight again. "You deserted me in such a hurry. . . . Because of that

battle-ax—right?" and as I remained silent, "Malwyda,"
he said, "you're unkind like Malwyda, there's another point
of similarity." "If that's the way you want it . . . This
chapel you mentioned, where is it located?" "Right here,"
he said, pointing down toward the floor, "underneath, in a
crypt. Just a few steps to descend . . . But no, Schwester,
you won't do it, I'm convinced you won't. . . ." "Would
you like to give me that key?" I asked, putting out my palm.
He lay the key there, reached back for it again—a pretext
for catching hold of my fingers. Through the glass windows
in the door I saw the chaplain in the midst of talking to the
medical officer; he was about to come in. I felt obliged to
pull my hand away; my wristwatch showed six o'clock, other
wounded patients were waiting for me. He thought I was
going to go away. "Stay," he said propping himself up on
his elbows, and he spoke in the same hot haste as at the
beginning, "there is something very important down below,
even appalling, I'll certainly not tell it to a Jesuit," and he
nodded toward the chaplain who, still in his conversation
with the medical officer, already had his foot in the door.
"But to you, to you, my angel . . ." And then after having
gazed into my eyes for a few seconds, holding the key to his
lips, his voice took on an almost lisping sound, like a child's
who is asking for something he knows only too well he isn't
supposed to have: "You could give me something—oh,
without any danger," and while I waited in the expectation
of extracting some piece of information or other that would
lie outside my province, "you know how important it is to a
man to be able to look at what he can't possess in any other
way." Lightly touching his finger to my blouse and with it
following the outline of my breasts: "There," he went on,
"they were a splendor in Malwyda." Though I had shrunk

back I hadn't been able to repress a faint quiver. "What harm could it do you?" he wanted to know, a tinge of Germanic heaviness in his tone. To this I had simply not reacted one way or another as any other girl in my position would have done. I even feigned a thoughtful air, my head cocked to one side, eyelids lowered, watching him from the corner of my eye. True enough, it couldn't do me any harm except getting me kicked straight out of the Red Cross if later on he ever happened to treat somebody else to confessions as candid as these he had made to me. That, however, seemed rather unlikely and in so far as I was alone concerned, it struck me as perfectly stupid to balk at such a naive fancy, coming from a maimed man. But such was Louise's intimidating influence over me that this favor he was asking, little though it was, seemed to me something I couldn't justifiably grant him unless it somehow accrued to the advantage of my mission. "Very well," said I, my cheeks aflame, "but first let me have that key." His face lighted up with gratitude and amazement; in his joy he seized both my hands and undertook to test the sincerity of my assent; he felt he didn't deserve it without unburdening himself of something rather more difficult to confess: "You don't know all the things I've done!" But I, disclaiming any eagerness to find out about what belonged to the fatality of events alone, I confined myself to asking what kind of important, appalling thing it was he'd alleged was to be found in the crypt. Here he stalled, gulping down a jigger of cognac; he doubtless needed to fortify himself in order to bring out this second series of things, less elegiac than the first. Apparently inspired by the promise I had just made him, he opened with a compliment, saying that I was not a girl to scare easily; and looking searchingly at me once again, he made some gestures meant to describe a compound. For several weeks, he began, he had been the man in charge of a camp of hostages. It hadn't been amusing, no, not for him either; and as a matter of fact he had soon received an order to send some Jewish families to Germany. Saying this he watched my face, on the lookout for the least hint of indignation I might show, and he sought to head it off by reminding me that it had been either carry out this order or incur a very stiff penalty. While I adopted an impassive expression so as not to make things worse than I felt they already were for him, he came to a detail which he probably interjected as an attenuating circumstance: he hadn't had the strength, he said, to ship the children out, and by persuading his second in command that there would be an advantage in hanging on to them, he had managed to spare them from deportation; and a little later he'd been able to confide them to that Italian chaplain, the condition being that the chaplain keep them on tap in case he needed to have them back. At this point I couldn't control reflexes that have been hereditary in us since the Revocation, and, speaking like a deaconness, "And so," I remarked, "you wouldn't have hesitated to send them off too had pressure been brought on you?" "What can you expect," he said, "I intended to survive." Once again I had the reply ready: "Is that what you call a soldier's honor?"—as if Louise had been prompting my lines to me, and I added an emphatic: "On and on, more victims, more innocents, the real presence notwithstanding." But, deep down, I hated him a lot more for his handsome face than on account of those poor children; an overpowering impulse originating within my flesh, untouched by the distresses he had been instrumental in causing, very nearly brought me to detesting the victims as a consequence of applauding his frankness. He had broken off and when I inquired after the fate of that chaplain, Von A. seemed to have lost the thread, mumbling something or other in German, pulling up his sleeves and plucking at the buttons on his shirt. He stretched his hand toward a bottle of alcohol, but something had inspired me to reach for it first, and once again our fingers came into touch. "How about a little massage?" he asked, smiling broadly, and with a wad of cotton I dabbed the nape of his neck and his temples while he sucked in deep lungfuls of the alcohol fumes, which enabled me to press him for an answer. Refreshed, he seemed to have less trouble recapitulating this recent part of the past, for from telling me what happened next he might, he may have thought, absolve himself in my eyes. Instead, without in the least realizing it, what he was to say brought me back down to earth with a jolt. After that? Having found out that the chaplain had hurriedly got the Jewish children out of harm's way by scattering them around in various convents, I sat up, literally relieved at being given something like a serious reason for paying Von A. more attention than I ordinarily should have. He was continuing, almost in a tone of recrimination. The S.S. had come to him demanding those children, a thorough investigation had been made. As a disciplinary measure they had sent him to the front, down at Anzio, and they'd shot the priest. He paused, holding his chin in his hand. He had put me on a track; was I going to follow it? join all the bright-eyed girls in their rut of wanting to do something useful? Were he to be willing to go on talking, Von A. would surely give me more clues. "A true martyr, that priest," I insinuated. Again he repeated that he'd been a spy, the only thing priest about him had been his cassock. I still didn't seem to grasp that it wasn't a question here of the clandestine activity of a brave man or a resistance hero but of an utter swindler: that under the cover of an act of charity he got himself paid a veritable ransom by the threatened families for each one of their children. Finally I began to feel as if he were deliberately trying to confuse everything in my mind when he started to refer to the relations he'd previously had with this Vittorio, as he called him, and whom he alleged to have belonged to the old Roman nobility; they'd first become acquainted at Bologna, at the university there. Having fallen madly in love with Malwyda, Vittorio had hoped to share her with him, and he'd opposed this, naturally; that Vittorio had held a grudge against him, and that at the moment the conflict between Ribbentrop and Ciano broke out, he'd worked against the Duce and the Führer, maneuvering between Ciano and the Vatican; that, to put it in a nutshell, he was a double-crosser. I was having difficulty following this sort of funeral oration; he suddenly halted it. Upset by a strong smell of ether coming from somewhere nearby, he said he could use a bit of fresh air and asked me to help him up. While I was wrapping my arm around his chest he swung his long legs out of bed and drew on a pair of boots. From off at the end of the ward the supervisor waggled a finger at him: the exercise hour was over and it would soon be time for roll call. Von A. nodded toward the French door opposite and when he was on his feet a slight tremble shook me at feeling his arm press mine. We headed for the door; it led out on to a balcony. Once outside, in the somewhat chilly air the rainstorm had left behind, under a troubled sky that swept all the way to a streak of turquoise just above the horizon, through a gap between two tall houses we saw the domes and the roofs of buildings lit by the flaming sunset. In the garden a fountain's jet mounted and sank back down into its basin between sprays of magnolias, and the measured tread of a pair of sentries walking on the gravel, the murmur of water, the subdued din of the city blended with the rumble of shellfire. A wall separated the hospital garden from the garden of an adjoining cloister. The bells there were ringing vespers just as Von A. reached the railing of the balcony and leaned upon it. His handsome features stood in silhouette against the sky, and I remained a moment with my hand tucked under his arm. We couldn't be seen from inside, having drawn the shutters over the windowed door after we'd come through it. Here, looking out over the Eternal City, the war, the events were blurred behind a keen but brief feeling of life's deliciousness. He shook his head in silence, his gaze fixed on the monuments of a vanished world, and seemed to have forgotten what he had been talking about when suddenly pointing to the dome of St. Peter's, he declared, "And to think I was supposed to kidnap that guy!" "Kidnap that guy?" I asked. "Which guy?" "Pius XII, just imagine! Take him to Nuremberg as a hostage!" and he began to giggle like a naughty child. Squeezing my shoulder, laughing harder, "That crazy Heidi suggested me as the man for the job. Clear the Pope out and set up Jupiter Capitolinus here in Rome!" And he was roaring so loudly that the sentries stopped and gazed up at the balcony; "Prego, silenzio, signore commandante!" one of them said, though both were grinning from ear to ear. "Yes, the name they had for it was 'Operation Apostata' and who knows but someday it may be pulled off," he went on merrily. "They proposed it and I said sure, I and a couple of others, it was a way to keep away from the Russian front, and besides I thought I'd be able to see Vittorio again. . . . That dirty little rascal made me believe we had Ciano's backing in this business and that he himself had taken holy orders only so as to keep a closer eye on Monsignor T. at the Vatican. . . . Obviously, such a piece of slapstick wasn't going to succeed, I never thought it would. But to work his way into my confidence he took it in great earnest, and in the meantime picked up information about other matters, important ones. . . ." He had stopped laughing; his elbows on the stone railing, he leaned forward and gazed down at the garden. "Poor stupid bastards, that's all we are." He flapped his hands emptily, then: "When I saw him the night before his execution he slipped me the key to the tabernacle. . . . The Holy Sacrament had been taken out of it, the chapel had been deconsecrated. . . . Therefore I could have access to the secret practiced there without having recourse to a priest." This last sentence had an odd sound. "Weren't you telling me just a short while ago about an influence of the real presence upon your relations with Malwyda?" "I said that to you . . ." he said dreamily, and one couldn't be sure whether he was speaking in the affirmative or interrogating himself. "Was it before Vittorio's arrest or after that you put those letters there?" He raised his hand to his brow as though he himself no longer saw the connection between this stage in his story and what he had told me at the beginning. ". . . Before, naturally. . . Before, of course." "So only he could have put them there, since he said Mass in the chapel?" "Yes, that's right. . . . But since I've come back from the front Mass is being said there again. . . . The real presence forbids me access to the tabernacle. . . . That was the trap. . . ." And still leaning on the balustrade, he bent his head down over his forearms. "A trap?" I said, "do you mean that the real presence is a trap?" and I hadn't restrained myself from stroking his hair with my fingertips. He straightened up like a shot. "Schwester," he said, "you'd be willing to testify in my behalf if they ever got hold of those papers?" "What papers?" "Schwester, there've never been any letters from Malwyda. . . ." "But. . ." I stammered, this time seized by a growing alarm. "There's nothing else there, down there, nothing . . . but the list of Jewish children. . . ." I was staggered. Inwardly, I was exulting. "Why not have said so right away? It's wonderful, the children can be restored to their parents!" "Parents? Their parents? . . . You're out of your mind, Schwester!" "But why, I want to know, why this wild story of letters entrusted to the Holy Sacrament, accusing yourself of the most awful—" "That list shows up and I hang. On the spot." And he buried his face in his hands. "Don't be downcast now," I said, "I'll do everything in my power to get those papers out of there." "And you'll never say a word of this to anyone, Schwester?" "I swear to it, on the Bible!" "No Schwester, oh no, don't swear that way!" Suddenly taking me in his arms and hugging me tight to him, "A couple of minutes ago . . . you promised me something, Schwester!" "I did promise you, it's true," I admitted, suddenly put off my bearings at seeing that he still had that detail on his mind. "Well, live up to your promise first, my angel, and then you can swear on the Bible. . . ." "You're quite right," I said, trying to wriggle out of his arms, "it's true that I never swear. . . ." "Your promise, my angel, your promise fulfilled will be the guarantee backing up your word." "Guarantee!" I exclaimed, breathless, "didn't I believe you without demanding any proofs. . . ." "You demand the key. . . ." "Only in order to help you!" "Only in order to get me hanged!" he shouted. "You simply say anything that comes into your head, like

that, and you've been lying all the time." "Lying! Lying?"
And he'd quickly let go of me; but it was to seize my head
between his two hands. He stared hard at me, his eyes in my
eyes. "You still think I'm lying?" "Yes you are, you are, you
are!" "You don't think me capable of having taken children
away from their mothers and fathers?" "Shut up!" "Of
having sent those mothers and fathers to the gas chambers?"
"Rubbish!" "You want them to hang me, you absolutely
want that?" and he lifted me up into the air as high as the
railing of the balcony. "Let go of me or I'll call for help!"
"One peep out of you and you'll end up on that gravel down
there," and he reached his hand to the neck of my blouse
and tore it open. "Not here," I said, "not here, we're being
watched!" But my blouse was open all down the front and
his broad hand touched my skin. "Little spy," he whispered,
thrusting his fingers into the hollow of my armpit, "phony
little nurse, powdered and perfumed to excite the wounded,
to get prisoners of war to talk, the hangman's little helper!"
Naturally, I was struggling and I slapped that lunatic; "Go
on," he sneered, "cut loose. Malwyda knew how to take care
of herself better than that," while my hands fluttered and
my fingernails glittered on his cheeks, trying to scratch him.
For the first time, a man dared do this to me and I cursed
not the hideous fate of those Jews torn away from their
children, but this alleged retribution from on high which
had been meted out to him at Anzio only to exacerbate his
urge to live. My hand soon grew still and, while my palms
were seeking his lips, the ties dissolved that bound me to this
world in which I had been taught to perform gestures of devotion, of self-sacrifice, of charity. When he had succeeded in
baring my breasts I quickly understood how much the same
they were to me, the wounded and the killed, the deported

and the persecuted, the tortured and the torturers, the atrocities and the punishing of those atrocities. At that very moment I saw my breasts lift, my nipples harden in spite of me, docile under these stranger's hands. They were the hands of an enemy, criminal and mutilated; and it would have been necessary that I, "the powdered and perfumed nurse," that I be taken totally and be totally had by him for the gravity of that hour to have been impressed upon me. But all this led nowhere. It didn't count.

Von A. had no sooner kissed the tips of my breasts than he lifted his head, an almost terrified look on his face. He clutched my hands. "Oh forgive me," he said, "forgive me, I didn't want that!" "What," said I, my excitement gradually draining away, "you didn't want that? When for once in your life you'd have nothing to be sorry about afterward. . . ." "Does it matter to you, Schwester? It's you, I'm afraid, who shall end up having had too much strength ever to be sorry for something. . . ." Then the shutters were thrown wide open. In the doorway stood the Italian medical officer, but behind him showed the white helmets of two hulking lads belonging to the American Military Police. The first Allied units had just penetrated into Rome and were searching everywhere for leftovers of Kesselring's forces. "A pure formality," the doctor said courteously. "What do you want with him," I burst out, speaking in their own language to the two M.P.'s who didn't have anything like an easygoing look. But their brick-red faces with the dark glasses remained impenetrable. "He's hardly begun his convalescence. . . ." and my glance swung to the medical officer. "They know it, Signora, for heaven's sake don't get yourself worked up." Von A. had turned around and looking their way, raising his eyebrows as if to say, "Already?" he showed his white teeth in a smile. And then a sort of dizziness came over me: for he had left my side and walked by himself back into the ward. Stopping between the two M.P.'s he waved at me. "We who aren't sorry about anything, our day will come too!" After that all I saw of him was his back, a willowy, lithe soldier on either side of him lending him a hand, leading him off. He himself walked with a bit of a stoop, his head pulled down close to his shoulders, swinging his long legs in somewhat jerky strides. I had stayed there on the balcony, my back turned to the city, my hands clinging to the edge of the balustrade. Inside, the same racket and merry-go-round had started up again between the various beds and I couldn't bring myself to cross through that ward again. An overpowering disgust stuck like a lump in my throat. I leaned over the garden: from Rome came tremendous pulsations of noise. The scene became misty and I discovered I was crying. I tidied my hair, slowly buttoned up my blouse, I was fairly quaking from rage when my fingers touched a flat metallic object in my bosom. It was the key to the tabernacle. And I drew it out, and I began to kiss it, passionately. This little object I'd forgot about, I squeezed it in my hand. Wasn't it somehow the token of a pact I'd just concluded with unknown powers. . . .